"I get to kiss you on tw

Kisses. Just kisses. But when had they ever been able to stop at just kisses?

She should protest. End this now.

Instead, Lydia breathed in the feel of having Ian this close to her. So close she caught a hint of his sandalwood aftershave that had occasionally clung to her skin after a night in his bed.

"When would those kisses happen?" Her eyes tracked his. "On what occasions?"

"Once on our wedding day. And once to seal the deal."

"As in...now?" She would not lick her lips even though her mouth went chalk-dry at the thought.

"Right now." His hand found the center of her back, his palm an electric warmth through the mesh fabric of her cover-up. "Do we have a deal, Lydia? One year together and I'll honor all of your terms."

Bad idea. Bad idea. Her brain chanted it as if to urge the words out of her mouth.

She nodded her assent.

* * *

The Magnate's Marriage Merger is part of the McNeill Magnates trilogy:

Those McNeill men just have a way with women.

Dear Reader,

Ian McNeill isn't about to let one matchmaking snafu tarnish his family's reputation. But he definitely didn't expect the matchmaker-gone-rogue to be his former girlfriend.

Reuniting with Lydia Whitney means unveiling her scheme to embarrass Ian's family. Except that seeing her again makes him remember all the ways they were very, very good together. Lydia, in the meantime, wants no part of Ian's misguided revenge. She has secrets of her own to protect. Secrets that could make Ian change his mind about everything he *thinks* he knows about their past...

Thank you for reading The McNeill Magnates and I hope you'll stay tuned for Cameron's book next month when *His Accidental Heir* releases as part of the Billionaires and Babies miniseries! Until then, please keep an eye out for my blogs and giveaways online by checking out my website at joannerock.com.

Happy reading,

Joanne Rock

JOANNE ROCK

—

THE MAGNATE'S MARRIAGE MERGER

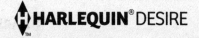

ISBN-13: 978-0-373-83846-2

The Magnate's Marriage Merger

Copyright © 2017 by Joanne Rock

This edition published by arrangement with Harlequin Books S.A.

For questions and comments about the quality of this book, please contact us at CustomerService@Harlequin.com.

® and TM are trademarks of Harlequin Enterprises Limited or its corporate affiliates. Trademarks indicated with ® are registered in the United States Patent and Trademark Office, the Canadian Intellectual Property Office and in other countries.

Printed in U.S.A.

Four-time RITA® Award nominee **Joanne Rock** has penned over seventy stories for Harlequin. An optimist by nature and a perpetual seeker of silver linings, Joanne finds romance fits her life outlook perfectly—love is worth fighting for. A former Golden Heart® Award recipient, she has won numerous awards for her stories. Learn more about Joanne's imaginative Muse by visiting her website, joannerock.com, or following @joannerock6 on Twitter.

Books by Joanne Rock

Harlequin Desire

Bayou Billionaires

His Secretary's Surprise Fiancé
Secret Baby Scandal

The McNeill Magnates

The Magnate's Mail-Order Bride
The Magnate's Marriage Merger

Harlequin Superromance

Heartache, TN

Promises Under the Peach Tree
Nights Under the Tennessee Stars
Dances Under the Harvest Moon
Whispers Under a Southern Sky

Visit her Author Profile page at Harlequin.com, or joannerock.com, for more titles.

For Heather Kerzner, who inspires everyone
she knows. I miss seeing you in person,
my friend, but I smile to think of all the people
you meet who benefit from having you in
their lives. Thank you for being a bright light!

One

"You found her?" Ensconced in his office at the McNeill Resorts headquarters in New York's Financial District, Ian McNeill glanced up from the file folder on his desk at the private investigator standing before him.

Ian had been back stateside for less than twenty-four hours when he'd gotten the message that the PI he'd hired two months ago had news for him. Ian's older brother, Quinn, had asked for his help to locate an anonymous Manhattan matchmaker who'd tried to pair their younger brother, Cameron, with a renowned ballerina. While that sounded harmless enough on the surface, the potential "bride" had had no knowledge she was supposed to meet Cameron, and it had caused a public scandal.

Bad enough in itself.

Except then the next day, the matchmaker responsible had closed up shop. Ian discovered within the week that the woman had been using a fake name and an assistant as a front to do most of her work. But despite a few leads, he hadn't had any luck finding the woman.

Until now.

"That's her." The investigator, Bentley, pointed to the closed file folder on Ian's desk. The guy was a former college roommate and someone he trusted. Bentley's specialty was digital forensics, but he took the occasional job outside the office if the case was interesting enough or, as in Ian's case, if the work was for a friend. With his clean-shaven face, wire-rimmed glasses and a faded pair of camo pants, Bentley looked more like a teenage gamer geek than a successful entrepreneur. "It's no wonder she used an alias for her matchmaking business. She's certainly well-known in Manhattan by her real name."

Ian slid the file closer, tapping a finger on the cover.

"The New York tabloids sold plenty of papers trying to guess her identity last winter after she paired up one of the Brooklyn Nets with that fashion blogger," Bentley explained. The mystery matchmaker had been responsible for a string of high-profile matches between celebrity clients and wealthy movers and shakers, and her success under an assumed name had the New York social scene all trying to guess who she was.

Curious, Ian leaned back in the cherry-red leather executive chair, manila folder in hand. The late-morning sun slanted in through the huge windows with a view of the river. Taking a deep breath, he flipped open the file to the papers inside.

Only to see an eight-by-ten glossy photo of his ex-lover's face on the top page.

Lydia Whitney smiled back at him with that Mona Lisa grin he'd fallen hard for a year ago—before she'd disappeared from his life after a huge argument.

Ian's blood chilled.

He sat up straight and waved the photo at his friend.

"What kind of sick joke is this?" He hadn't told Bentley about his brief affair with Lydia, but the guy specialized in unearthing digital trails. He must have stumbled across some link between them in his investigation.

"What do you mean?" Bentley frowned. Shifting positions, he leaned forward to peer at the folder as if to double-check what Ian was looking at. He shoved the wire-rimmed glasses up into his shaggy dark hair. "That's her. Lydia Whitney. She's the illegitimate daughter of that billionaire art collector and the sexpot nurse he hired before he died. Lydia's mother sued the family for years for part of the inheritance."

Tension kinked Ian's shoulders. A tic started below his right eye.

"I know who she is." *Damn. It.* Just looking at the picture of Lydia—the Cupid's bow mouth, the dimples, the pin-straight dark hair that shone like a silk sheet flowing over one shoulder—brought the past roaring back to life. The best weeks of his entire life had been spent with those jade-green eyes staring back into his. "I'm asking why the hell there's a photo of her here."

"Ian." Bentley straightened. When his glasses shifted on his head, he raked them off and jammed them in the front pocket of his olive-green work shirt. "You asked me to find the matchmaker who used the name of Mallory West. The woman who hid behind an alias when she worked for Mates, Manhattan's elite dating service. That's her."

The news sank into Ian's brain slowly. Or maybe it was Bentley's expression that made him take a second look at the file in his lap. His former college roommate was a literal guy, and he wasn't prone to pulling pranks. And he appeared serious about this.

Gaze falling back on Lydia's flawless skin, Ian flipped past the photo to see what else the file contained. The first sheet was a timeline of the events of last February when "Mallory West" had paired Cameron McNeill with ballerina Sofia Koslov. There were notes about Mallory's assistant, Kinley, who'd admitted that Mallory was an alias but refused to identify her boss. Then there were pages of notes about Kinley's whereabouts, including photos of Kinley meeting with Lydia at various places on the Upper East Side—where Ian knew Lydia lived.

"Lydia Whitney is the mystery matchmaker?" As he said the words aloud, they made a kind of poetic sense.

Lydia had ended the most passionate affair of his life when she'd discovered Ian's photo and profile were on a dating website while they were seeing each other. He'd understood her anger, but mistakenly assumed she would listen to his very reasonable explanation. He had not posted the profile or created the account. He'd given cursory permission to his grandfather's personal aide to do so after a heated argument with the old man, but had heard no more about it after that day.

Grandpa Malcolm McNeill was so determined his grandsons should marry that he'd since written the condition into his will. None of his grandsons would inherit their one-third share of the global corporation he'd built until they'd been married for at least twelve months. That stipulation had come last winter, prompting Cameron to find a bride with a matchmaker, leading to the fiasco with Sofia Koslov. But the pressure to wed had started long before that. And it had resulted in Ian's offhanded agreement to allow his profile to be listed on a dating website.

But Lydia didn't care about his explanation. She'd been furious and had cut off all contact, accusing him of betrayal. What if she'd gone into the matchmaking business—at the very same agency his grandfather had used—to spite Ian? In the months after that, Ian had indeed received some odd suggestions for dates that he'd ignored. Could Lydia have been behind those, too? Anger rolled hot through his veins. Along with it, another kind of heat flared, as well.

"I was surprised, too," Bentley observed, moving closer to the window overlooking the river and Battery Park. "I thought Mallory West would be someone with more Park Avenue pedigree. An older, well-accepted socialite with more connections among her clientele." The investigator rested a shoulder on the window frame near Ian's bookcase full of travel guides.

It didn't matter that he could get maps of every country on his phone when he traveled for work. Ian liked seeing the big picture of a foldout map, orienting himself on the plane ride to wherever it was he headed to oversee renovations or development work on resorts all over the globe.

"She used to work as an interior designer," Ian observed lightly, tossing aside the file before he gave any more away about the relationship he hadn't shared with anyone. "Do you know if she still does?"

He needed to think through his response to this problem. He had planned to hand over Mallory West's real identity to Vitaly Koslov—the ballerina's father—who had every intention of suing the matchmaker for dragging his daughter through unsavory headlines last winter. But now that Lydia was the mystery matchmaker? Ian needed to investigate this more himself.

"Yes. Throughout the year she worked as a matchmaker, she continued to take jobs decorating. Since she walked away from the dating service, she is back to working more hours at the design business, but she still volunteers a lot of her time with the single mothers' network I mentioned in the notes."

"Single mothers?" Frowning, Ian opened the file again and riffled through it.

"Moms' Connection. She gives a lot of money to the diaper and food banks." Straightening, Bentley backed up a step. "Anyway, mystery solved, and I've got an appointment in midtown I can't miss. Are we good here?"

"Sure. I'll have my assistant send the payment." Setting aside the file, Ian shoved to his feet and extended a hand to his friend. "I appreciate the time you put into this."

Bentley bumped his fist. "Not a problem. I'd forgo the payment if you could get me a meeting with your brother Cameron."

"Cam?" Ian frowned, thinking his friend must have confused his brothers. "Quinn's the hedge fund manager. Were you thinking of doing some investing?"

"No. It's Cameron I'd like to meet with. Word is, he's working on a new video game and I've got some ideas to speed graphics. I'd prefer to work with an independent—"

"Done." Ian wasn't ready to dive into a discussion full of technojargon, but he knew his younger brother would speak Bentley's language. Cameron was the family tech guy since he owned a video game business in addition to his role in McNeill Resorts. "I'll put him in touch with you."

Seeing his friend out the door, Ian returned to the photo of Lydia Whitney he'd left on the window ledge. He felt the kick-to-the-chest sensation all over again. He needed to see her in person to get to the bottom of this. He'd thought they were finished forever when she broke things off last spring. But clearly, there was unfinished business between them.

Pivoting on the heel of one Italian leather loafer, Ian pressed the intercom button on his phone to page his assistant. In seconds, Mrs. Trager appeared in his doorway, tablet in hand.

"Yes, Mr. McNeill?" The older woman was efficient and deferential in a public setting, but she'd been with him long enough that she didn't pull punches when they worked together privately.

"I need to find a consulting gig, and I'm willing to take a pay cut to secure the right one. It doesn't matter where it is in the world, as long as you can get me onto a project where Lydia Whitney is providing the design services."

Despite the highly unusual request, Mrs. Trager didn't even blink as she tapped buttons on the digital tablet. "I just read in an architectural trade that Ms. Whitney recently committed to Singer Associates for a hotel renovation on South Beach."

"Good." He knew Jeremy Singer well. The guy only bought highly specialized properties that he liked to turn into foodie havens. "I'll call Jeremy myself. Once I speak to him, I'll let you know how soon I'll need a flight."

"Very good." His assistant tucked the tablet under one arm. "I forwarded you an article about the property."

"Thank you." Settling back into the chair behind his oversize desk while Mrs. Trager closed the door behind her, Ian had a plan already taking shape.

He had met Lydia on a shared job site a little over a year ago. Working closely together to develop a unique property had meant they spent long hours in each other's company. Once Lydia realized who she'd be working with, she might very well try to detach herself from the Singer project, but she was too much of a professional to simply walk off a job site.

Which gave Ian at least a few days to figure out what in the hell was going on with Lydia Whitney.

She'd taken some anonymous revenge against him, it seemed, and he had every intention of calling her on it. But first things first, he needed to slip back into her world in a way that wouldn't send her running. Once he had her in his sights, he would figure out how to exact a payback of his own.

He'd never considered himself the kind of man who could blackmail a woman into his bed. But with the surge of anger still fresh in his veins at this betrayal Ian planned to keep all his options open.

Tilting her head back, Lydia Whitney savored the Miami sun. The weather was still beautiful at eight o'clock in the morning before the real heat and humidity set in. Seated at her outdoor table at the News Café on Ocean Drive, she had a breeze off the water and a perfect cup of coffee to start her day before her first meeting for the new interior design job on South Beach.

The swish of the ocean waves rolling onto the shore, along with the rustle of palm fronds, was a

persistent white noise. Foot traffic on both sides
of Ocean Drive was brisk even though June was
a quieter time for the tourist area. The tables near
her were both empty, so she felt no need to rush
through her coffee or her splurge breakfast of almond brioche French toast. No one was waiting
for her table. She could linger over her newspaper,
catching up on the Manhattan social scene.

Perhaps, if she was a more dedicated interior
designer, she'd be studying the other recent hotel
renovations on South Beach so she could ensure
she approached her new job with a singular, dis-
tinctive style. But she didn't work like that, prefer-
ring to let her muse make up her own mind once
she saw the plans and the proposed space.

Instead, Lydia read the social pages with the
same avid interest that other women devoted to
watching the *Real Housewives* series. She soaked
in all the names and places, checking to see who
was newly single or newly engaged. It was all
highly relevant because, in her secret second job,
Lydia still did some moonlighting as a matchmaker
to Manhattan's most eligible bachelors and bach-
elorettes. It was a job she couldn't seem to give up,
no matter that she'd had to leave the high-end dating service that had allowed her to work under the
alias of "Mallory West."

There'd been a bit of a scandal last winter, forcing Lydia to leave town and take a brief hiatus from

matchmaking. Her life had been too full of scandals to allow for another, so she'd buried herself in design work for the next few months, ignoring the tabloid speculation about the true identity of Mallory West. But she'd missed the high drama and the lucrative second income of the matchmaking work, especially since she donated 100 percent of those profits to a charity dear to her heart.

"More coffee, miss?" A slim blonde waitress in a black tee and cargo shorts paused by her table, juggling an armful of menus and a coffeepot.

"No, thank you." Lydia switched off the screen on her tablet by habit, accustomed to protecting her privacy at all times. "I'm almost finished anytime you want to bring the check." She should be early for her first meeting, even if she hadn't done a lot of design homework to prep for it.

Singer Associates, the firm that had hired her to overhaul the interior of the landmark Foxfire Hotel, had been good to her over the years. The firm had hired her for the job where she'd met Ian McNeill, she recalled. Perhaps that had been the only time where a Singer Associates job had a snag attached, since her disastrous affair with Ian had broken her heart in more ways than one.

But that certainly hadn't been Jeremy Singer's fault.

Stuffing in one last bite of the almond brioche French toast, Lydia promised herself to arrive earlier for breakfast tomorrow so she could people watch on Ocean Drive. Most of her potential matchmaking clientele fled to the Hamptons or Europe this time of year, not Miami. But there were always interesting international travelers in South Beach, no matter the season. Not to mention the fresh-faced models who were a dime a dozen on this stretch of beach. And wealthy men were always interested in models and actresses. It couldn't hurt to keep her ears and eyes open for prospects as long as she was in town.

Retrieving her leather tote from the chair beside her, Lydia paid her bill and dialed her assistant back in New York as she walked south on Ocean Drive toward the Foxfire Hotel.

Traffic crawled by as tourists snapped photos of the historic art deco buildings in the area. The cotton candy colors of the stucco walls wouldn't work as well anywhere but at the beach. Here, the pinks and yellows blended with the colorful sunrises and sunsets, while the strong, geometric lines balanced the soft colors. The Foxfire Hotel had lost some of its early grandeur in misguided attempts to update the property, with subsequent owners covering up the decorative spandrels and fluting around doors and windows. Her contract with Singer Associates—the new owner—had assured her those details would be recovered and honored wherever possible.

"Good morning, Lydia." Her assistant, Kinley, answered the call with her usual morning enthusiasm. The younger woman was at her desk shortly after dawn, a feat made easier by the fact that she sublet rooms in Lydia's Manhattan apartment for a nominal fee. "Did you need anything for your morning meeting?"

"No. I'm all set, thanks. But it occurred to me that I could collect some contacts while I'm down here for our second business." Pausing outside the Foxfire, she knew Kinley would understand her meaning and her desire to be discreet. "I wondered if you could see who we know is in South Beach this month and maybe wrangle some fun party invites for me?"

"Are we ready to dive back into the dating world?" Kinley asked. In the background, Lydia heard her turn down the brain-tuning music that her assistant used while she was working.

"I think we've lain low for long enough." Lydia had quit working with the bigger dating agency when Kinley had paired a prominent client with a ballerina who was unaware she'd landed on a list of potential brides.

The snafu hadn't been Kinley's fault; it was caused by the ballerina's matchmaker, who'd listed her client in the wrong database. The incident had made the New York social pages, implicating "Mallory West" as potentially responsible. Instead of drawing attention to herself and her business, Lydia had simply withdrawn from the matchmaking world, mostly because the prominent client had actually been Ian McNeill's younger brother, Cameron. Lydia hadn't wanted to draw the attention of her former lover just when she'd finally been starting to heal from their breakup.

And from the loss of the pregnancy she'd never told him about. The punch to her gut still happened when she thought about it. But the ache had dulled to a more manageably sized hurt.

"Music to my ears." Kinley's grin was obvious in her tone of voice. "I've been keeping our files up-to-date for just this moment so we'd be ready to go when you gave the okay."

"Excellent. Look for some South Beach parties then." She checked her watch. "I'll touch base with you after the meeting."

"Got it. Good luck." Kinley disconnected the call.

Lydia entered the building, her eyes struggling to adjust to the sudden darkness. The hotel had been closed since the property had changed hands, and was a construction site. Lights were on in the lobby, but some remodeling efforts were already underway with the space torn down to the studs.

"Right this way, ma'am." An older man dressed in crisp blue jeans and wearing a yellow construction hat gestured her toward the back of the lobby where plywood had been laid over the sawdust on the floor. "You must be here for the new owner's meeting." At her nod, he extended a hand. "I'm Rick, the foreman."

She quickened her step, approaching to shake his hand and blinking at the bright white light dangling from an orange electric cord thrown over a nearby exposed rafter.

"Nice to meet you." She'd learned early in her career to make friends with the site supervisor wherever possible since that person usually had a better handle on the job than whatever upper level manager was put on the project.

"We've got you set up at a table in the courtyard." He gestured to two glass doors in the back leading to a broad space of smooth pavers and manicured landscaping open to natural sunlight. "Just through there."

"Great." She straightened the strap on her leather tote and smoothed a hand over her turquoise sheath dress. She wished she'd found a restroom before she left the News Café so she could have touched up her lipstick and checked her hair; she hadn't expected the conditions at the Foxfire to still be so rough. "It's a beautiful day to enjoy the outdoors."

"For another hour, maybe." Rick chuckled to himself. "You New Yorkers all like the heat until you're here for a few days in the summer."

Yes, well. There might be a smidge of truth to

that. She'd probably be melting this afternoon. Thanking him, Lydia pushed through the glass door on the right, her eye already picking out a wicker chair off to one side of a large wrought iron table. She was glad to be early so she could pull over the wicker seat and save herself from sitting on wrought iron for however long this meeting lasted.

A small water feature burbled quietly in the open-air courtyard, sending up a soft spray of mist as it tumbled over smooth rocks and landed in a scenic pool surrounded by exotic plantings. Dwarf palms mingled with a few taller species that attracted a pair of squawking green parrots. High up, at the top of the building, a retractable canopy over part of the space dimmed the sun a bit without blocking it completely.

"Lydia." She turned her head sharply to one side to find the source of the familiar baritone.

She hadn't heard that voice in over a year. It couldn't be…

"Ian?" She felt that breathless punch to her gut again, harder than it had been this morning when she'd thought of her lost pregnancy.

Ian McNeill stood in the far corner of the room beside a Mexican-style tea cart laden with silver ice buckets and cold, bottled drinks, his strong arms crossed over his chest. His slightly bronzed skin that hinted at his Brazilian mother's heritage made his blue eyes all the more striking. His dark hair was short at the sides and longer on top, still damp from a morning shower. He was impeccably groomed in his crisp dark suit, gray shirt and blue tie.

Ian McNeill. The lover who'd broken her heart. The man who'd kept his profile on a matchmaker's site while he dated her, prompting her to go into the matchmaking business just so she could try her hand at sending horrible dating prospects his way. She'd outgrown the foolish need for vengeance after she'd lost their baby. So it had been an accident when she'd paired Ian's brother with that famous ballerina.

How much did Ian know about any of that?

"Nice to see you, Lydia," he said smoothly, approaching her with the languid grace of a lifelong athlete. "A real pleasure to be working with you again."

His eyes held hers captive for a long moment while she debated what he meant by "pleasure." The word choice hadn't been an accident. Ian was the most methodical man she'd ever met.

"I didn't know—" She faltered, trying to make sense of how she could have taken a job where Ian McNeill played any role. "That is, Jeremy Singer never told me—"

"He and I agreed to exchange peer review services on a couple of random properties—a recent idea we had to keep our project managers on their toes and revitalize the work environment." Ian brought a bottled water to the table and set it down before tugging over the wicker chair for her. "I was pleased to hear you were in line for this job, especially since you and I work so well together."

He held the chair for her. Waiting.

Her heart thrummed a crazy beat in her chest. She could not take a job where she'd be working under Ian.

Oh, God.

She couldn't even think about being *under Ian* without heat clawing its way up her face.

And, of course, those blue eyes of his didn't miss her blush. He seemed to track its progress avidly as the heat flooded up her neck and spilled onto her cheeks, pounding with a heartbeat all its own.

When the barest hint of a smile curved his full, sculpted lips, Lydia knew he wasn't here by accident. It had all been by design. She wasn't sure how she knew. But something in Ian's expression assured her it was true.

She opened her mouth to argue. To tell him they wouldn't be working together under any conditions. But just then the glass doors opened again and the job engineer strode into the room with Rick, the foreman she'd met briefly. Behind them, two other women she didn't know appeared deep in conversation about the history of the Foxfire, comparing notes about the size of the original starburst sign that hung on the front facade.

Lydia's gaze flicked to Ian, but the opportunity to tell him what she thought about his maneuvering was lost. She'd have to get through this meeting and speak to Jeremy Singer herself since she couldn't afford to walk off a job.

But there was no way she could work with the man who'd betrayed her.

Even if he affected her now as much as ever.

Two

Doing his damnedest not to be distracted by the sight of Lydia's long legs as she sat on the opposite side of the room, Ian paid close attention in the Foxfire meeting, appreciating the favor Jeremy Singer had done by letting Ian step in at the last minute. Having worked with the resort developer on a handful of other projects over the years, Ian understood the man's style and expectations, so he would offer whatever insights he could on the job site. Since launching his own resort development company on a smaller, more exacting scale than his grandfather's global McNeill Resorts Corporation, Ian wasn't normally in the business of overseeing other people's buildings when he was in a position to design his own. Yet he did enjoy having a hand in specialty public spaces like the foodie-centered resort Singer planned for the revamped Foxfire.

One of the drawbacks of running his own business was less day-to-day focus on his clients' concerns, building restrictions and the inevitable permit nightmares. Being on-site now and again gave him renewed awareness of the obstacles in his work. So this brief stint at one of Jeremy Singer's buildings was no hardship.

And the payoff promised to be far greater than the sacrifice of his time.

Ian's gaze slid to Lydia's profile as the meeting broke up. She remained in her seat on the opposite side of the room, speaking to a woman in charge of indoor air quality on the job site. The room was full of people who would only play a limited role in the renovation, but Ian had wanted to attend the meeting and get up to speed as quickly as possible. The enclosed courtyard was crowded, too, ensuring Lydia couldn't walk out the door before he caught up with her.

Her turquoise dress skimmed her slight curves and was accented by a belt with a thin tortoiseshell buckle emphasizing a trim waist. The hem ended just above her knee, showcasing her legs in high-heeled gold sandals. Her straight dark hair slid over one arm as she turned, still in conversation with the other woman, her dimple flashing once as they continued their animated talk. Clearly, the two of them knew each other, but then again, they moved in a small world of elite professionals.

Would Lydia try to leave without speaking to him privately? He didn't think so. She was not a woman to mince words. And while he'd caught her off guard—clearly—by showing up here without her knowledge, she'd had two hours during the meeting to consider her course of action. She would confront him directly.

The idea tantalized far more than it should have. She'd walked away from him. Worse, she'd meddled in his affairs without his knowledge. Even that, he might have forgiven. But how could she extend her vengeance to his family? She'd matched his brother Cameron to an oblivious stranger. The meeting—and Cameron's impulsive proposal in the middle of a private airport—had been caught on film by a dance magazine that was doing a special on the ballerina and would-be bride. The episode put their older brother, Quinn, in the awkward position of trying to smooth things over in the media to placate the woman's furious and embarrassed father.

Lydia had been responsible for all of that, and Ian wasn't about to forget it. Even if things had worked out in the end when Quinn fell hard for the ballerina himself. The two were now engaged. Happy.

Ian exchanged pleasantries with the site manager as the rest of the group filed out through the glass doors and back into the main building, leaving him and Lydia alone in the interior courtyard. A water feature gurgled in the space as yet untouched by the remodel.

The babble of water over a short rock wall softened the impact of the sudden silence. Shoving to his feet, Ian stalked around the wrought iron table to where Lydia sat, gathering her things and tucking a silver pen into the sleeve inside her leather tote bag.

"I need to speak with you privately," she informed him, slinging the tote onto one shoulder as she met his gaze.

He'd forgotten how green her eyes were. He remembered staring into those jade depths while the two of them stood in a languid pool off the Pacific on a beach in Rangiroa, just north of Tahiti. He'd thought then that her eyes matched the color of the water—not really emerald green or aqua that day, but a brilliant green.

He'd thought a whole lot of foolish things then, though. A mistake he would not be repeating.

"I figured you might." He inclined his head. "My car is outside."

For the briefest moment, she nipped her lower lip. *Uncertain? Or unwilling?*

Or tempted? Ah...

"We might as well work while we talk," he explained. He didn't want her to think he planned to cart her off and ravish her at the first opportunity, the way he once would have after a tedious two-hour meeting. "Traffic should be reasonable at this hour. We can drive over to Singer's inspiration hotels and take a look around."

"Of course." She pivoted on her heel and preceded him toward the exit. "Thank you."

His eyes dipped to the gentle sway of her hips in the turquoise silk, the hint of thigh visible in the short slit at the back of her skirt. He didn't recognize the dress, but the thighs were a different story. He and Lydia had been crazy about each other, tearing one another's clothes off at the slightest opportunity. One time, they'd barely made it to an outdoor shower stall on their way up to his villa from the beach.

Now her hair had grown longer, reaching to the middle of her back. Last year, it had been cut in a razor-sharp line across the middle of her shoulder blades. Today, it draped lower, the ends trimmed in a V that seemed to point to the sweet curve of her lovely ass.

He reached around her to open the door for her, leading them into the Miami sun, grown considerably warmer over the last two hours. Once outside, he flicked open the top button on his shirt beneath his tie, knowing full well this noontime excursion wasn't going to be all about work and knowing with even more certainty that his rising temperature had more to do with the woman in step beside him than the sun above him.

"This way." He pointed toward the valet at the next hotel over, grateful the attendant behind the small stand noticed Ian and sent one of the younger workers into the parking garage with a set of keys.

No doubt his rented convertible BMW would be driven out soon enough. He ushered Lydia to one side of the street while they waited, his hand brushing the small of her back just long enough to feel the gentle glide of silk on his fingertips and the warmth of her body underneath.

The South Beach scenery—palm trees, exotic cars, brilliant blue water and beach bodies parading to and from the shore on the other side of the street—was nothing to him. Lydia had his undivided attention.

"You just happened to be in Miami?" She turned on him suddenly, the frustration that had been banked earlier finding fresh heat now that they were alone. "On a job that has nothing to do with McNeill Resorts or your personal development company?"

He caught a hint of her fragrance, something

tropical that stood out from the scent of the hibiscus hedge behind her.

"I am here to see you." He saw no need to hide his intentions. "Although even I didn't realize until recently how much unfinished business remained between us."

"So pick up the phone." She bit out the words with careful articulation, though her voice remained quiet. "There was no need to fly fifteen hundred miles to ambush me on my project."

"*Our* project," he reminded her, letting the "ambush" remark slide. "And I saw no sense in calling you when you purposely went into hiding after we left Rangiroa." He'd been furious that she'd blocked him in every way possible, giving him no access to her unless he wanted to be truly obnoxious about seeing her. He refused to be that guy who wouldn't give up on a woman who wanted nothing to do with him.

"You knew how I felt about public scandals." She hugged her arms around herself for a moment, eliciting an unwelcome twinge of empathy from him.

With a very famous father and a mother who was unrepentant about going after his billions, Lydia had received way too much media attention as a child and straight through her teen years. Her parents were the kind of media spectacle that the tabloids cashed in on again and again. In

Lydia's eyes, all her mother had done was to destroy Lydia's relationships with her father's family.

"You had no reason to believe I would ever make our affair public." He spotted the silver Z4 rolling out of the parking garage and pointed out the vehicle to her. "You know me better than that."

"I only thought I knew you, Ian."

She didn't need to say any more than that for him to hear the damning accusation behind the words as they headed toward the car.

Tipping the valet service, Ian grudgingly allowed one of the other attendants to close Lydia's door behind her, not surprised the thin veneer of civility between them was already wearing thin. He'd cared deeply about her and he was sure she'd once felt the same about him. The raw hurt of tearing things apart had left them both full of resentments, it seemed.

Indulging those bitter emotions wasn't going to get him what he wanted, however. His objective remained to find out what she was doing messing with his life and his family's welfare through her so-called matchmaking efforts.

"Do you mind having the top down?" he asked. They'd shared a Jeep with no top to roam around the French Polynesian island a year ago, but the stiff-shouldered woman in his passenger seat today bore little resemblance to the laughing, tanned lover of those days.

"It's fine." She reached into the leather tote at her feet and retrieved a dark elastic hair band that she used to twist her hair into a tail and then a loop so the pieces were all tucked away somehow. "Maybe having some fresh air blowing around this conversation will help us keep our tempers."

He pulled out of the hotel parking area and onto Ocean Drive.

"Either that or the Miami heat will only fire things up more." The question was would it result in hot frustration? Or hotter lust?

Seeing her arranging her long, dark hair had already affected him, and he knew his brain had stored away the image to return to later.

In slow motion.

"I prefer to think optimistically." She leaned back in her seat as he slowly drove north through heavy traffic that still didn't come close to the grid-lock that plagued this city in the evenings. "So where are we going?" She swiveled in her seat. "There are more of the traditional art deco buildings to the south of us, I think."

"That may be, but I've got a spot in mind that will give us the lay of the land first." He needed to get her alone. Somewhere private where he could focus his full attention on the conversation.

"The lay of the land?" She shielded her eyes and peered ahead of them. "Florida isn't exactly famous for its high ground."

"That's what penthouses are for." He steered into the right lane where the street began to widen even as the traffic didn't seem to lessen.

"A penthouse?" She shifted to face him in her seat, her eyes narrowing. "You can't be serious."

"You'll like this, trust me."

"Not *your* penthouse?" she pressed.

Was that a hint of nervousness in her voice? Either she didn't trust him or she didn't trust herself. He tucked that intriguing thought away.

"I took the penthouse suite at the Setai." He pointed to the luxury hotel looming just ahead of them. "It comes with access to a private rooftop pool. We can speak up there and take in the whole art deco district at the same time."

"You're in the penthouse at the Setai?" She turned her attention to the front of the hotel as he steered the BMW toward the waiting valet. "One of the ten most expensive suites in the known world?"

"Is it?" He didn't usually indulge in that kind of extravagance when he traveled, but then, this wasn't his usual brand of business trip. "Then it's a property that will appeal to the designer in you."

He wondered if she would have agreed if it weren't for the private valet and concierge service already giving them the red carpet treatment as the car pulled up. Lydia's attention was on the attendant who opened her door. Another attendant offered to help with her tote as he discreetly asked what she might require.

That alone made the suite pay for itself, because in the end, Lydia got on the private elevator with Ian and headed to the fortieth floor where they could be alone.

Lydia, you have lost your mind.

She'd been so distracted by the gracious service as she entered the famous hotel that she'd somehow ended up speeding her way toward Ian McNeill's private penthouse suite. She wished it was as simple as the designer in her taking a professional interest in a world-class luxury space, the way Ian had suggested. But she feared that it was more complex than that. Ian had swept her right back into his world today, imposing his will on her work environment, and then staking a claim on her private time, too.

Yes, she'd wanted to speak to him privately. But damn it, that didn't necessitate a trip to a hotel suite with a one-night price tag as high—higher—than what many people paid for an automobile.

"Ian." She took a deep breath before turning to face him.

Just then, the elevator doors swished open, revealing the most gorgeous, Asian-inspired decor imaginable, framed by views of the sparkling sapphire Atlantic out of window after window.

"Wow." Her words dried up.

As a student of architectural design, she did indeed find a lot to savor about the rooms, the layout and the exquisite care taken to render every surface beautiful. She'd read about this suite before in an effort to keep up-to-date on the world's premiere properties, so she'd seen photos of the Steinway in the foyer and—oddly—recalled reading about the absolute black granite in the shower. She guessed the penthouse was close to ten thousand square feet with the double living rooms, a full dining room for ten people and multiple bedrooms. As she walked around the space in admiring silence, her eyes lit on the private terrace overlooking the beach below.

Ian had gotten ahead of her somehow. No doubt she'd been lost in her own thoughts as she'd circled the living areas of the penthouse. But she spotted him in the lounge area of the terrace, speaking to waitstaff who'd set up silver trays in a serving area under a small cabana. White silk had been woven and draped through a pergola, creating a wide swath of shade over the seating.

In all of this exotic, breathtaking space, Ian himself still seemed to be the most appealing focal point. In his crisp blue suit custom-tailored to his athletic frame, he drew the eye like nothing else. His whole family was far too attractive, truth be told. She'd seen photos of his Brazilian mother, who'd left Ian's daredevil father long ago. They'd made a glamorous couple together. Liam McNeill had the dark hair and striking blue eyes of his Scots roots, resulting in three sons who all followed a Gerard Butler mold, although Ian had a darker complexion than the others.

If the gene pool hadn't been kind enough there, Ian was also relentlessly athletic. He'd sailed, surfed and swum regularly while they worked on the hotel property in French Polynesia, and the results of his efforts were obvious even when he was wearing a suit. When he was naked...

Blinking away that thought, she forced her feet forward, refocusing her gaze on the glass half wall surrounding the huge terrace forty stories up. She breathed in the salty scent of the sea that wafted on the breeze while Ian excused the servers.

Soon, she felt his presence beside her more than she heard him. He moved quietly, a man in tune with his surroundings and comfortable enough in his own skin that he never needed to make a noisy entrance. Damn, but she didn't want to remember things that she'd liked about him.

"You were right," she admitted, relaxing slightly as she stared out at the limitless blue of the ocean. "In bringing me here, I mean. It's stunning. Although calling this space a penthouse hardly does justice to how special it is."

"I enjoyed seeing your reaction to it." Out of the corner of her eye, she saw Ian's posture ease.

One elbow came up beside hers on the half wall as he joined her at the railing. "Being on the design end of so many projects—and experiencing all the headaches that entails—makes it easy to forget why we enjoy what we do. Then, you see a place like this where they got everything right. It's a reminder that not every project is about a bottom line."

She hesitated. "Yes. Except how many people will ever get to enjoy it?"

"Not enough," he agreed easily. "But if we're inspired, we'll do a better job with properties like Foxfire. And that's an attainable vacation for a lot of people." Turning from the view, he gestured toward the cabana where the food trays waited.

A few minutes later, she had settled herself on a long, U-shaped couch that wrapped around a granite coffee table under the shade of white silk, a plate of fresh fruit and cheese balanced on one knee. Ian poured them each a glass of prosecco even though she'd already helped herself to a bottle of water.

She'd forgotten how extravagantly he lived. While her father had been extremely wealthy, her mother hadn't always been. After suing Lydia's father's estate, she'd eventually taken great joy in overspending once her settlement came through, but by then, Lydia had moved on to her own life. Her father had left her a small amount that she had put toward the purchase of her Manhattan apartment, but his legally recognized children had inherited his true wealth. Besides, Lydia had spent her childhood perpetually worried that her mother would squander their every last cent on frivolous things, so Lydia maintained a practical outlook on finances, careful never to live above her means.

Still, who wouldn't enjoy a day like this?

"You mentioned you wanted to speak to me privately after today's meeting," Ian reminded her as he handed her the sparkling prosecco in a cut crystal glass. A single strawberry rested at the bottom. "Why?"

"Isn't it obvious?" She sipped at the bubbles and set the drink aside. "Ian, I can't work with you on this project."

He'd removed his jacket to expose the gray silk shirt beneath. His muscles stretched the fabric as he moved, reminding her of the honed body beneath.

"You're a professional. I'm a professional. I think we can put aside personal differences for the sake of the project." His expression gave away nothing.

Old hurts threatened to rise to the surface, but she kept a tight rein on those feelings.

"Don't you think you're diminishing what we once meant to each other to call our breakup a 'personal difference'?" Her chest squeezed at all that she'd lost afterward.

One eyebrow lifted as he met her gaze. "No

more than you diminished what we meant to one another by playing matchmaker for me afterward, Mallory West."

Three

He knew.

Lydia felt her skin chill despite the bright South Beach sun warming the thin canopy of silk over-head. For a long moment, she only heard the swoosh of waves far below the rooftop terrace, the cry of a few circling gulls and her own pounding heart.

"That's what this is about?" she managed finally, shoving off the deep couch cushions to pace the lounge area near the hot tub. "You found a way to play a role in the same design project as me so you could confront me with this?"

"You don't deny it then?"

"I played a childish game of revenge after we

broke up, Ian. You caught me. But it hardly did any damage when you never actually went on a date with any of those women." She'd started her matchmaking career out of spite. She wasn't proud of it, but she had been in a very dark place emotionally.

"No. But I also didn't post my profile on that matchmaking site, as I tried to tell you from the start. My grandfather's assistant ran the photo and the profile after Grandad twisted my arm about marriage." Ian unfolded himself from his place on the couch to stand, though he did not approach her. "So my grandfather personally reviewed your suggestions that I date...those women." His jaw flexed with annoyance.

She'd sent ridiculous dating suggestions to the manager of Ian's profile. She'd been furious to discover he had an active profile on a popular dating website while she'd been falling in love with him. And his refusal to understand why she was upset, his infuriatingly calm insistence that it meant *nothing*, had shredded her.

She'd been tired and overly emotional at the time, but she'd credited it to her broken heart and deep feelings for him. Only a week later, she'd discovered she was pregnant.

"I was hurt by your cavalier dismissal of my concerns." She moved toward the glass half wall, taking comfort from the sight of the ocean and the relentless roll of incoming waves. "It was petty of me."

"My grandfather was the one who was disappointed." Ian stalked closer, his broad shoulders blocking her view of the water. "But your temporary anger with me doesn't explain why you deceived my younger brother into thinking he was meeting a potential bride, only to have the woman turn out to be completely unaware of his existence." Cool fire flashed in Ian's eyes as he studied her. "It's one thing to lash out at me. But my family?" He shook his head slowly. "No."

"That was an accident." Her temples throbbed with the start of a tension headache as this meeting quickly spiraled out of control. "A genuine accident. Although it didn't help that Cameron signed a waiver saying he didn't care if the matches had been vetted—"

"He clicked a button online to agree to that. Hardly the same as signing something."

"But my assistant explained to him—"

"An assistant who impersonated you, by the way."

Which was something Lydia regretted tremendously. But she'd handed off Cameron McNeill as a client because she hadn't been ready to face Ian's brother with her emotions still raw where Ian was concerned. By the time she'd realized the error in Cameron's match, it was too late to fix it. Jumping in to deal with the aftermath would have meant facing Ian in person—and she hadn't been ready for that at a time when she'd only just started to recover emotionally from the miscarriage.

"I am sorry about that." She pivoted to face him head-on. "I really weighed the options for getting involved after I realized what had happened. But would you really have wanted me to step in when Quinn and Sofia had already announced an engagement? I didn't want to undermine whatever was happening between them by drawing even more attention to the mismatch with Cameron." She'd followed the courtship of Sofia Koslov and Quinn McNeill closely and it had been obvious to her from the photos of them together that they were crazy about each other. "And yes, I was trying to protect my identity. My work had become very important to me by then."

"Very important or very lucrative?"

"Both." She refused to be cowed by him. Straightening to her full height she narrowed her gaze. "I put one hundred percent of the profits after expenses from matchmaking toward a very worthy cause."

"Moms' Connection."

His quick reply unsettled her. How much did he know about her life in the past year? Her shoulders tensed even tighter.

"How did you know that?"

He rested an elbow on the railing, relaxing his posture.

"That's actually one of your less well-guarded secrets. I hired a friend to learn the identity of Mallory West in the hope of sparing Cameron any further embarrassment." Ian shrugged a shoulder. "And to spare Sophia Koslov further embarrassment, since Cameron's potential bride turned out to be the love of Quinn's life."

"I read about that. I'm glad that some good came out of the situation." She hesitated a moment before deciding to press on. "You hired someone to find me?"

What else did he know about the last year of her life? Worry knotted her gut, but she had to hope that the confidentiality of her medical records had withstood his investigation.

"I wasn't expecting to find *you*, Lydia. I hired someone to track Mallory West." His words were clipped. "I can't begin to describe my surprise at discovering you'd had a hand in my affairs ever since you broke things off with me last summer."

"You gave me no choice," she reminded him, remembering the sting of seeing his smiling, handsome face on a friend's page of potential matches on the Mates International dating site. "You not only betrayed me, you did so publicly. If we'd been dating in Manhattan instead of Rangiroa, I can only imagine the fallout." She needed to leave now.

To escape whatever dark plans he had in mind by following her to South Beach and insinuating himself back into her life. "But thankfully, that wasn't the case and the rumors of our affair died quickly enough."

Pivoting on her heel, she retrieved her tote bag, prepared to request an Uber.

"I just have one question." Ian followed her across the private terrace, his arms folded over his broad chest as he walked.

"I'm listening." She found her phone and clutched it in one hand.

"Why do all the profits go to a charity benefiting single mothers?"

It was on the tip of her tongue to lie. To tell him that it was a way to help women like her mother, who'd allowed being a single parent to turn her into a bitter person.

But she knew that he wouldn't believe her. He knew her better than that, understood the complex and difficult relationship she had with her mom.

"I met a few women who worked with the group." That was true. Still, her mouth went dry and the heat was beginning to get to her. This whole day was getting to her.

No. Ian McNeill was getting to her.

Those intensely blue eyes seemed to probe all her secrets, seeing right through her.

"How? Where?" he pressed, even as he gestured her toward a seat on the couch again.

He lowered himself to sit beside her as she wondered how much he already knew. She didn't want to equivocate if his personal investigation had already revealed the truth.

"At a support group for single mothers." Her eyes met his. Held. "I attended a few meetings in the weeks after our affair." She had been so touched by those women. So helped by their unwavering support. She took a deep breath. "That was before I lost the pregnancy and...our child."

Ian felt like he'd stepped into the elevator shaft and fallen straight down all forty stories.

"What?" He thought he'd been shocked to discover Lydia was the woman behind Mallory West. Yet the blow he'd felt then was nothing compared to *this*. "You were pregnant when you ended things between us?"

She'd been so fierce and definite. So unwilling to listen to any explanation even though Ian hadn't done a damn thing to post that stupid profile. And all the time she'd been carrying his child? A new anger surged—putting all the other frustrations on the back burner.

How could she hide that from him?

"I didn't realize it at the time. But yes." Lydia unclenched her hand where she'd been holding her cell phone. Setting it carefully aside on the table beside their untouched lunch, she shifted her tote to the outdoor carpet at her feet. She seemed unsure where to look, her eyes darting around the terrace without landing on any one thing. "I realized later that the pregnancy hormones were probably part of the reason why I reacted so strongly to finding your profile online. But it never crossed my mind that I could be pregnant for another week, and then—"

"We were so careful." His mind went back to those long, sultry nights with her. Lydia all wrapped around him in that villa with no walls where they could look straight out into the Pacific Ocean, the sea breezes cooling their damp bodies after their lovemaking. "Every time we were careful."

"There were a couple of nights we went in the water," she reminded him, nibbling on her lower lip. "The hot tub once. And the ocean…remember?"

Her green eyes brought him right back to one of those moments when he'd been looking into them as a rainfall shower sprayed over them in the outdoor Jacuzzi. Her delicate hands had smoothed over his shoulders, nails biting gently into his skin as he moved deeper inside her.

"Yes." His voice was hoarse with how damn well he remembered. "I recall."

She pursed her lips. "Maybe one of those times.

I don't know. But I can tell you that I tested positive when it occurred to me I might be pregnant and then—"

"I had a right to know." That part was only just beginning to really take hold in his brain, firing him up even more. "When you first found out, you should have told me."

"Because things had ended so happily between us?" she retorted, her brow furrowed. "Ian, you didn't even deny that you were going to date other people. You said your family wanted you to find a wife."

"That could have been you." He articulated the words clearly, restraining himself when he wanted to roar them for all of South Beach to hear. "And I didn't deny your ludicrous accusation about dating other people because I had no intention of dating anyone but you."

Hell, he'd fallen in love with her. He'd been ready to propose, thought they knew everything about each other there could be to know. And it had insulted him in the very fiber of his being that a woman he cared about so much could think so poorly of him that he would advertise himself for dates with other women. Clearly, they hadn't known each other as well as he thought. He'd been too damn impulsive and mistook intense—very intense—passion for love.

Later, he'd forgotten about his grandfather's

plan, pure and simple, because he'd been caught up in his work and in Lydia. Plus, they'd been a million miles from home and the pressure of the McNeill world.

She went so quiet that he wondered what she was thinking. Instead of asking, he helped himself to a swig of the prosecco they'd left out on the table, trying to settle his own thoughts.

"As I said, I was probably operating under the influence of pregnancy hormones. I've spoken to a lot of other mothers since then, and they say it's a powerful chemical change." She surprised him with her practical admission, especially after the matchmaking games she'd played last summer.

Maybe time had softened her initial anger with him. Or showed her that he might not be fully to blame for his grandfather's matchmaking transgression.

"Setting aside the fact that you never informed me about our child—" he took a deep breath as he willed himself to set it aside, too "—can you tell me what happened? Why do the doctors think you miscarried?"

He had a million other questions. How far along had she been? Had she ever considered reaching out to him before she'd lost the baby? What if the pregnancy had gone to full term? Would she have ever contacted him?

That last question, and the possibility that the answer was no, burned right through him.

"The cause was undetermined. My doctor assured me miscarriages happen in ten to twenty-five percent of pregnancies for women in their child-bearing years, so it's not that unusual." She laid a hand across her abdomen as she spoke. An unconscious gesture? "The most common cause is a chromosome abnormality, but there's no reason to believe it would happen to me again."

Hearing the vulnerability in her voice, seeing it for himself in her eyes, made some of the resentment ease away.

"I'm sorry I wasn't there with you." He reached to take her hand resting beside him on the couch.

Her skin felt cool to the touch despite the heat. She stared down at his fingers clasping hers, but didn't move away from the connection.

"I didn't handle it well." She retrieved her bottle of water and took a long drink. "It might have been hormones, but the sadness was overwhelming. But I spent a lot of time with the mothers' group I told you about. Being with them helped me to heal."

A row of misters clicked on nearby to provide water to the exotic flowers tucked in a planter by the doors to his suite. The cool spray glanced over their skin before the water evaporated in the Miami sun glinting off white stone walls all around the rooftop terrace.

"That's why you support this group now—Moms' Connection." He tried to fit the pieces together in his mind to figure out what she'd been through in the past year.

"Yes. I met some incredibly strong women who inspired me. Seeing their efforts to help other single mothers made me realize how petty it was for me to meddle in the matches that were being sent to you." She hesitated. "I started to put more effort into really matching up people and I discovered I was good at it."

Sliding her hand from his grip, she smoothed it along the hem of her dress, straightening the fabric.

"So you kept at it and used the funds to help the group that helped you." His vision of her shifted slightly, coming into sharper focus. "And what happened with Sofia Koslov and my brother was, as you say, a genuine accident."

"Yes. I shouldn't have taken your brother on as a client, but by that time, Kinley was filling in for me often. I was away for several weeks last winter doing a job for a singer who moved to Las Vegas for an extended contract and wanted me to design her new home." Lydia picked one red strawberry from a plate on the table. "But the profits from the matchmaking work were doing a lot of good for the mothers' organization by then. I didn't want to let my support of a good cause lapse. I still don't."

She bit into the strawberry, her lips molding to the red fruit in a way that made his mouth go dry.

"You must be aware that Sofia Koslov's father is an extremely wealthy and powerful man. He allowed my family to investigate the matter of Mallory West's identity since she's now engaged to Quinn, but when he finds out who you are, he has every intention of suing." Ian hadn't told a soul about discovering that Lydia was behind the debacle.

He hadn't even told his two brothers, which didn't sit particularly well with him. But he'd been handed an opportunity to bargain with this woman and he wasn't about to lose it.

Initially, he'd entertained fantasies about leveraging his position for revenge. But now he knew that his relationship with Lydia was far more complex than that. There was still an undeniable spark between them—and a connection that went deeper than just the attraction. Otherwise, the news of her losing a pregnancy wouldn't have affected him like a sledgehammer to his chest.

Which meant he was going to be bargaining for something more than sensual revenge.

"I had hoped now that Sofia is marrying your brother later this month, her father wouldn't want to draw public attention to the matchmaking mishap." The worry in Lydia's eyes was unmistakable as the ocean breeze tousled her dark hair where it rested on her shoulders.

Ian buried any concern he might have had about her feelings. She certainly hadn't taken his into account when she hid the news of his child from him.

"Vitaly Koslov strikes me as a man who does not forget a slight to his family." Ian respected that. He wasn't inclined to let a slight to his go unchecked either. "But I have a suggestion that might help you avoid a civil suit and restore your matchmaking business."

"You do?" The hope that sparked in her gaze ignited a response in him.

This was a good plan. And it was going to solve problems for them both.

"You are aware that, due to familial pressure, I am in the market for a wife?" The terms of his grandfather's will had caused him no end of grief in his relationship with Lydia, after all. "Last summer, my grandfather had already started to apply pressure to wed, but this winter, he created legally binding terms in a rewritten will. In order to retain family control of my grandfather's legacy, my brothers and I each need to marry for at least twelve months."

"But you already have your own successful business—"

"Keeping McNeill Resorts in the family is about legacy, not finances." He wouldn't allow his third of the company to go to strangers. Cameron and Quinn felt the same about the family empire.

"I can help you find someone, if you'd like a private consultation." Her words were stiff and formal.

Did she honestly not guess his intent? Or was she bracing for the inevitable?

"That's kind of you. But I'm perfectly capable of choosing a temporary wife for myself."

"You're taking over that task from your grandfather?" She arched an eyebrow at him, challenging.

With just one fiery look, she reminded him how good it was going to be when he touched her again.

And he would touch her again. Soon.

"Definitely. My search just ended, Lydia." He allowed himself the pleasure of skimming a knuckle down her bare arm. "You will solve both our problems if you agree to be my wife for the next twelve months."

Four

"He proposed to you?" Lydia's assistant, Kinley, squealed in Lydia's ear late that night during a conference call to catch up on business back in New York.

With her feet tucked beneath her on the sofa while she ate her room service salad, Lydia shifted her laptop on the coffee table to reduce the glare from the reading lamp. Kinley's hazel eyes were huge, her face comically close to her webcam as she gestured for Lydia to hurry up with her story.

"Yes." Stabbing a cherry tomato with her fork, Lydia tried to ignore the butterflies in her stomach that the memory invited. Why on earth would she feel flattered to be part of Ian's scheme to use her in order to deceive his grandfather? But the fluttery feeling in her belly had been undeniable—both when Ian suggested marriage, and now as she related the story to Kinley. "He means it strictly as a business arrangement."

Although when he'd asked her, he'd been trailing the back of one knuckle down her cheek, making her think about how good they were together and what the man's touch could do to her. So she hadn't said no as quickly as she would have wished.

"And he would protect you from scandal if it comes to a lawsuit over the match between his brother and Sofia Koslov?"

Lydia watched her assistant on the computer screen. Back in New York, Kinley's pen hovered over a crossword puzzle in the newspaper, a habit she'd developed once she started skimming the social pages for any interesting leads in the matchmaking world.

"He made it clear he would keep my name out of the headlines and negotiate with Vitaly Koslov if there are legal repercussions." The Ukrainian entrepreneur was the founder of the mega-successful start-up, Safe Sale, and was worth billions. Lydia had read all about him after the bad press she'd received for the misfire with his daughter's matchmaking experience.

And Ian would swoop in and save her. Just like

she'd once dreamed a romantic hero would do for the woman he loved, back when she still believed in happily-ever-afters. Foolish, foolish visions for her to indulge when she'd grown up with the most cynical of parents whose relationship was a continual power struggle.

"So what did you say?" Kinley pressed, tapping her pen impatiently against the newspaper.

"I turned him down in no uncertain terms, at which point he reminded me that if I wanted Mallory's identity kept secret, I should give his offer more careful consideration." Remembering that thinly veiled taunt still made her fume hours afterward. At the time, she'd been too angry to trust herself to speak.

She'd called the elevator and let the Setai's attentive concierge put her in a car the hotel offered her as Ian's guest. No doubt, they would have escorted her all over town if she wished—a reminder of how far apart their lifestyles had always been. For all that her father had been a wealthy man, Lydia worked hard to pay her own bills, refusing to fall into her mother's role of bilking others in order to lead an extravagant lifestyle.

"I'll admit it's not exactly the proposal every girl dreams of." Kinley began tapping the pen against her cheek, her lips pursed thoughtfully. "But still. Ian McNeill?" She whistled softly. "A woman could do worse for herself."

"Marriage isn't a competitive sport." Lydia twirled the hotel bathrobe tie around her finger, agitated at how the day had unfolded—start to finish. "I'm not trying to find the richest or most prestigious partner."

"I was thinking more along the lines of the best looking." Kinley grinned shamelessly. "He's seriously hot." She ran her finger over the screen of her phone before flipping it toward the camera to show Lydia a photo of the man himself. "C'mon, Lydia. You can't deny that he's super yummy."

Those blue eyes were magnetic. No doubt.

But the picture wasn't nearly as appealing as the temptation she'd faced today when he stroked a hand along her cheek or told her he wished he'd been there with her when she lost their baby. Those moments had rattled her resolve far more than the vision of his strong shoulders or disarming smile.

Perhaps the idea of a temporary marriage to Ian wouldn't sting so much if she hadn't once let herself imagine a very real marriage with him. Sure, they'd only dated for six weeks, but it had been an intense affair that dominated both their lives. Things had escalated fast.

"That's hardly a good reason to enter into a complicated relationship." If anything, the sensual pull she felt for him was a strike against the idea. She was so drawn to him that it would be easy to let herself confuse attraction for caring again.

And *that* she could not allow.

"Hmm…twelve months of having the world at your feet and a gorgeous, well-respected billionaire to fend off your enemies and keep you safe?" Kinley shook her head, her expression serious for the first time all evening. "I will go out on a limb and say there's more at work here than you're telling me."

Caught.

Lydia shot her an apologetic smile. "Ancient history better forgotten than relived." She took a deep breath. Lydia had resolved to move on after she shared this crazy turn to her day with Kinley. Now it was time to live up to her promise. "But on to more important things. Did you find some parties I should be attending to meet potential clients or possible matches for our current clients?"

She wanted to spend her time helping the cause dear to her heart by raising money for women who really needed it. That meant no more wallowing in regrets over how things had turned out between her and Ian. She'd find some other way to protect her business, even if he revealed her identity as Mallory West to the powerful Vitaly Koslov.

"I did. I'm emailing you a list as soon as I lock down a few more contacts for you. I want to be sure you don't have any trouble getting into any of the events. There are a few European royals in town this month, so invitations are in high demand."

She paused. "Although I'm sure Ian McNeill would get the red carpet treatment at all of these places."

Thinking back to that over-the-top penthouse suite at the Setai, Lydia didn't doubt it. He moved in the circles Lydia's mother had never managed to penetrate. And although there'd been a time when Lydia didn't care about acceptance into that kind of elite, she'd begun to see the benefits if only for the sake of Moms' Connection.

"I'm sure he does. But since he won't be attending any of these functions with me, I will wait for you to work your magic on my behalf. Just do whatever you can with my father's name." She refused to feel guilty about that since her father had been a committed philanthropist. He would have applauded Lydia's efforts, she felt certain.

Not for the first time, she wished she'd had more time with him growing up, but she'd been her mother's bargaining chip from the day of her birth, withheld from her dad whenever her mother was unhappy with him.

Which meant she didn't see him often. And when she did, her mother was close at hand, making sure to take her share of the billionaire's attention.

Finishing up her business with Kinley, Lydia ended the video call and closed her laptop. She was staying at the Calypso Hotel close to the Foxfire, in a small room with an ocean view. The suite needed updating desperately, but as she padded across the black-and-white tile floor to the sliding glass door overlooking the water, she admired the same view that Ian had in his gargantuan spread just twenty blocks away. Her surroundings indoors might pale in comparison, but with the ocean waves lapping the shore below, providing a soothing music despite the stressful day, she too could enjoy the most priceless kind of beauty.

Breathing in the soft, salty air, she tried to let the Atlantic work its magic. But deep down, she knew she hadn't escaped Ian McNeill's marriage offer simply by walking out of his suite. He'd allowed her to leave, no doubt so she could mull over the idea—rage against it—and slowly realize how thoroughly he had her back against the wall.

Revealing her as the woman behind Mallory West threatened to derail all her hard work with Moms' Connection, turning her life back into another scandal-ridden media circus when she'd worked so hard to put the antics of her mother behind her. Furthermore, even if she managed to keep the matchmaking business afloat and somehow turn a profit in spite of all the media attention, she would have Vitaly Koslov to contend with, a powerful business mogul with the power to bankrupt her on every front.

Right now, she could afford to live in Manhattan and run a business she enjoyed. Losing a civil suit to Koslov might ruin her financially for years to come. All she had to do to avoid those consequences was put herself in Ian McNeill's hands for one year. She simply had to wed the man who'd left her heart with the deepest scars.

Just seeing him for one day had threatened to rip those old wounds open again. She couldn't possibly go through with it.

So, turning to enter her hotel room and slip between the sheets for the night, Lydia knew she'd have to refuse him when he asked her again. Because not for a moment did she think he'd dropped the idea of a temporary union between them.

Ian McNeill wasn't a man to take marriage lightly. Even the cold-blooded, contractual kind.

Nodding a greeting to the desk attendant at the Calypso Hotel shortly before dawn, Ian checked his watch as he took up a spot near the main elevators. It was one of South Beach's aging art deco—era properties. Standing on the huge tile inlay featuring a gold starburst design, Ian pulled his phone from his pocket to check his stocks for the day, but in reality all he could think about was Lydia.

It was a risk to surprise her. But when she'd ended their conversation prematurely the day before, she must have known he would find a time to renew their discussion. Sooner rather than later. She was a woman of habit and that would serve him well now. He hoped. He remembered how much she had enjoyed swimming first thing in the morning when they were working together in the islands of Tahiti. He'd accused her of being a mermaid with her daily need to return to the sea, but even when he'd been bleary-eyed from working late the night before, he never missed a chance to swim with her. For safety purposes, he'd told her, and not just because he enjoyed the occasional chance to slide a hand beneath her bikini top or wind the wet rope of her hair around his hand and angle her sea-salty lips for his kiss.

When the elevator sounded its dull chime, he slowly looked up. The doors opened and Lydia strode into view. His gaze fell on her long, shapely legs, the hem of her black mesh tunic revealing a hint of thigh.

"Ian?" Her voice tugged his attention higher, pulling his focus to her green eyes and creamy skin devoid of makeup.

With her hair scraped back into a ponytail, she looked every inch the part of his earthy, warm-hearted lover from last summer. He had to remember that she hadn't been the woman he thought, that he'd been wrong about her, or he might have swept her up into his arms and ridden the elevator back up to her hotel room to remind her how good they were together in at least one respect.

Sex. Raw, sensual, mind-blowing sex.

His pulse ramped up at the steamy memories, so much so that he had to shut down those thoughts and focus on the present or his plan would be doomed before he even started.

"Hope you don't mind if I join you." Ian tucked his phone back into the pocket of the cargo shorts he'd slid on over his swim trunks.

She halted in front of him abruptly. Then, eyes sliding to the desk attendant, she stepped closer. Probably she did it to minimize the chance of being overheard.

Ian liked the opportunity to breathe in the scent of her—the lavender fragrance of the detergent she washed her clothes in and a subtle perfume more complex than that.

"What on earth are you doing here?" She glanced over her shoulder. "You realize most of the consultants working on the Foxfire are staying in this hotel? What will they say if someone sees us together at this hour?"

"They'll think we had a whole lot more fun last night than they did."

Last night, he'd paced the floor of his penthouse suite for far too long, thinking through every aspect of a contract marriage and what details he should include in the paperwork.

In the end, she would sign. But she wasn't going to like him forcing her hand, and that bothered him more than it should have.

"And that doesn't concern you? I happen to enjoy a hard-earned reputation as a professional." Her clipped words and the high color in her cheeks told him he'd gotten under her skin in record time.

"If you don't want anyone to see us together, we might as well hit the beach. Take refuge in the water." His hand itched to touch her. To rest on the small of her back and steer her out the door, across the street and onto the soft sand. But he had to be careful not to push or she could dig her heels in about his suggestion and delay the whole thing.

Now that he'd made up his mind and seen the benefits of a union between the two of them, he couldn't think of one damn reason why he should delay.

After narrowing her green eyes at him for an instant, she pivoted on her wedge sandals and strode toward the exit.

He caught up to her in two long steps, holding the door wide for her before as they headed out onto Ocean Drive, which was strangely quiet in the predawn dark. There were more joggers on the beach than bathers; a few runners kicked up sand as they pounded past them.

"It'll be quieter down here." He pointed out a stretch of the shore where no beach loungers had been set up yet, a spot free from any hotel guests.

In fact, he'd claimed the location for them earlier when he'd ordered a cabana and sunrise breakfast.

Lydia apparently didn't notice his preparations, however, instead appearing too absorbed in her frustrated march toward the water, her feet churning through the sand at breakneck pace.

The horizon was starting to smudge from inky black to purple as she reached the shoreline and kicked off her shoes. Then she yanked the black mesh cover-up off and over her head. Mesmerized by her silhouette as his eyes adjusted to the light, Ian watched as she ran into the surf and made a shallow dive under an oncoming wave.

He retrieved her clothes and put them in the cabana where he removed his own shorts and tee, stacking them off to one side out of the way of a server still setting up a tea cart full of trays for their breakfast.

Then Ian sprinted into the ocean after Lydia, seized with memories of other times they'd done this. They'd had plenty of games they played in the water, from him grabbing an ankle and tracing the long line of her leg up to the juncture of her thighs to races of every kind. He didn't think she'd appreciate the former, so he settled for the latter, pacing her as she executed perfect butterfly strokes through the salty water.

With the horizon turning lavender now, he could see her better. Her creamy skin glinted in the soft light each time her arm broke the surface. Only when they were far from the shore did she stop short to tread water.

"You're insane," she accused softly, even though she seemed significantly calmer than when she'd been on her march toward the water. With her dark hair plastered to her head and the long ponytail floating around her shoulders, she looked so beautiful and so damn familiar that it hurt.

"To swim in a dark ocean before the sun rises? Or to brave your wrath and swim beside you when I know you're angry?"

Her huff of frustration rippled the water in front of her. "To propose marriage when we have so much…unhappy history. So much frustration between us. It's crazy and you know it." She swatted aside a drifting clump of seaweed.

"I'm a practical man, Lydia. And by now, I'm sure you've had enough time to realize how practical my suggestion is." He'd wanted her to have cooling off time yesterday, but he guessed she'd been awake as long as he had last night, thinking about the possibilities.

"Practical?" She rose up on her toes to move out of the way of a swell coming toward them. "Ian, we aren't some royal couple needing to secure the family line or keep the castle in the clan. Marriage isn't supposed to be a line item in a business deal."

"And it won't be." He took her hand before the

next swell rolled over them. "Come this way so you can touch the bottom."

Even that simple touch—his grip wrapped around her fingers in the cool water—sent a flash of undeniable heat through him. Judging from how fast she pulled back, he would guess she felt it, too.

"I'm fine," she argued despite the goose bumps along her arm.

"You're cold." He pointed to the shore where their server had left a small hurricane lamp burning on the table. "You see the cabana? I ordered some breakfast for us. Let's dry off and talk about this reasonably before the next wave drags you under."

"We're having breakfast there?" She shook her head slowly, but began swimming toward shore. "I have the feeling you could have had the free buffet at the Setai."

He laughed.

"Maybe so. But my hotel lacks your company. A situation I hope to change once you agree to my proposal."

She stopped swimming. But they were so close to the shore now, they were able to stand and walk side by side the rest of the way. She'd stopped arguing, which he took as a positive sign. So he kept his peace for now, shortening his stride to stay beside her as they moved closer and closer to their destination. The all-white tent was closed on three sides but open to the water, the domed roof making it look like something out of *Arabian Nights*.

She nibbled her bottom lip, then released it slowly before shooting a sideways glance his way. "You're really serious about this."

"You doubted it?" He passed her a towel from the stack an attendant left near their clothes.

"Not really." She squeezed the water out of her long ponytail and let it drip onto the sand. "I guess I hoped maybe you were just trying to scare me with the threat of Koslov's lawsuit. Make me regret what I'd done by interfering in your romantic life with the matches I suggested."

She'd sent him suggestions for dates with a reality TV star renowned for her diva-ish behavior and an ex-girlfriend she knew he disliked for using his name to get ahead in her career for long after they'd broken up.

"No." Moving to the sideboard where the food had been set up, he poured them both coffee. "Although I won't deny I let myself imagine all kinds of inventive sensual blackmail once I found out you were the woman behind Mallory West."

She clutched the towel tighter to her lovely body as he set the mugs on the bistro-size table. When she said nothing, he waited another moment to continue, letting his words sink in. He wasn't going to pretend that he wasn't attracted.

Or that he wouldn't act on it.

"But after we had the chance to speak yesterday, I realized you were under an incredible amount of stress at that time, and I regret not being there for you." It made his chest go tight thinking about her alone and losing their child. *Their child.* He had to swallow down the lump in his throat before he could continue. "No matter what else happened between us, you should have known you could contact me."

He hadn't forgiven her for keeping the baby a secret in the first place, but he hated that she'd been through that by herself.

She sank into her chair at the table, stirring sugar into the coffee he'd placed in front of her. She made no protest when he set a plate of food before her, the stoneware loaded down with fruits and cheeses he knew she liked. The scent of eggs and bacon wafted from the warming trays as he prepared a plate for himself and a smaller, second one for her.

"So you didn't suggest marriage as a punishment." She gave him a lopsided smile and slid her arms into the black mesh bathing suit cover-up.

"Far from it." He pulled on his linen buttondown shirt and took the seat across from her, letting his knee brush hers under the table and seeing the jolt of awareness in her eyes. "I think a marriage between us could have all kinds of added benefits."

Five

A shock of heat radiated out from that one spot where their legs brushed, seizing Lydia's attention faster than any words. How easy it would be to heed that impulse, to fall under the spell of simmering attraction until she was powerless to resist it. Of course, it didn't help that she remembered so many other times when she'd allowed this very sensation to carry her away, pulling her into his arms to answer the hunger only he could fill.

Urging herself to be stronger than that, she shifted her legs away from him under the table, crossing one knee over the other to put herself farther out of his reach.

"I'm not sure it's fair of you to resort to under-handed tactics to convince me we should try this crazy scheme of yours." Taking a sip of her coffee, she focused on the pink sun rising past the horizon, bathing them both in warm light.

The beach was still quiet at this early hour with a smattering of tourists more focused on the famed nightlife than the joys of the early morning. About twenty yards away, a fisherman cast a line and waited to see what was biting, his chair half in the surf. A few interested birds stalked him, sensing the possibility of an easy meal.

"Underhanded?" Ian straightened, as if rearing back from an undeserved slight. But then a smile curved his sculpted lips, sliding right past her boundaries. "Under the table, maybe. But hardly underhanded."

"You know what I mean." She stabbed a half strawberry with her fork and ignored all the nerve endings urging her to listen to him, to let him woo her back where her body would love to be. "If we can't hash out terms logically, it's not a good idea to start wielding seduction as a weapon."

"Lydia," he began, his tone gently chiding. "Seduction was a very rewarding part of our re-lationship. I'd never want it to be anything but a pleasure."

He didn't move any closer as he spoke, but somehow the air thickened around them as if he'd grazed against her again. Hearing the word *pleasure* on his lips wasn't good for her defenses.

"Then let's keep it out of the negotiations." She spoke through gritted teeth, she realized, and forced herself to take a breath.

"Of course." He finished his eggs and moved his plate aside, leaning his elbows on the table.

The breeze off the water blew through his dark wavy hair, which was beginning to dry. He was impossibly handsome with his deeply bronzed skin and blue eyes.

"Good." Relaxing a little, she hoped she could still reason with him. "Then we can discuss alternatives to the marriage plan."

"The only alternative is me revealing Mallory West's identity to the world, Vitaly Koslov included." Ian lifted the coffee carafe to pour her more.

Her stomach cramped. He was perfectly serious. Ian might be the peacemaker within the McNeill family, brokering middle ground between his conservative older brother and his playboy, techno-genius younger sibling, but that didn't mean Ian himself ever gave ground. More often than not, the other McNeills let themselves be guided by Ian's position.

"That will ruin any hope of resurrecting my matchmaking career. Aside from the personal loss, I would be saddened by the missed opportunity for the world of good it's doing for so many people," she reminded him, unable to enjoy the fresh fruit on her plate when her nerves were wound tight. She didn't want to lose her ability to give back to Moms' Connection and the women who'd helped her through the darkest time of her life.

He shrugged with a pragmatic air. "Sometimes we make sacrifices for the things that are most important to us."

How could he be so cavalier about love? "And you don't care if I look at marriage to you as sacrificing myself?" Maybe she'd hoped some small part of him still cared about what they had meant to each other once.

"We are both offering something to get what we want." He tapped the table as if jabbing home his point. "I prefer to focus on the positives."

"Like you getting around your grandfather's terms for the will?"

"Precisely." He reached to take her fork from her plate and spear a grape. He then lifted it, offering it to her. "And you avoid a civil suit while growing your business." He paused, fork hovering in midair. "Among other benefits."

That damnable heat returned to her skin. How could she have forgotten how easily he tampered with her ability to think clearly?

"So you mentioned. But I'm not going to suddenly take up where we left off just because we sign on for a year together." She withdrew the fork from his fingers and set it down again, unwilling to play romantic games with him. "Not that I'm seriously considering this idea at all, Ian. If anything, I'm still trying to figure out how to get out of my contract with Singer Associates so I can leave South Beach and the Foxfire project altogether."

"I would never expect you to pick up where we left off a year ago." His gaze was steady and direct. He appeared sincere. "I know the heat is still there, but it would be up to you if we did anything about it—plain and simple."

Her heart beat faster just talking about it. How would she ever find enough strength to resist the man day in and day out for a whole year if she were to actually consider going through with this?

She really didn't want to lose her matchmaking business because the proceeds did so much good for the charity she cared about. Confused and flustered, she stood abruptly.

"I can't do this again." She shook her head, wishing she could shake off the old feelings crowding out reasonable thought. "The first time hurt too much."

Retrieving her towel, she wanted to retreat before she did something foolish. Like throw her arms around his neck and press herself against him, or drag him deeper into the cabana and peel off his clothes.

"Please." Ian stood with her, a hand darting out to capture hers, linking their fingers with an ease from their past relationship. "My grandfather had a heart attack last winter after the debacle of Cameron proposing to Sofia."

Ian's touch curved around her elbow, gentle but firm.

"I'm sorry. I didn't know."

"It happened while he traveled abroad. In China, in fact. That helped us to keep it quiet."

She softened a little, knowing how much Malcolm McNeill meant to all of his grandsons. She recalled how Ian had told her about his fond memories of the older man throughout his childhood.

With the sun just above the horizon now, pink and orange light spilled over them, a spotlight just for them. Ian's fingers caressed the back of her arm lightly and she could feel her resistance ebbing away with the tide.

"Will he be okay?" She read between the lines. If something happened to Malcolm McNeill and Ian had not fulfilled the terms of the trust, the family would lose control of McNeill Resorts.

"We hope so. He had a pacemaker put in and his doctors say he's doing well. But Gramps wouldn't let us take him to see his physician in the States yet until he's certain he can control any rumors spreading about his health."

They stood just inside the cabana's shelter, her bare toes curling in the sand as Ian's fingers stroked lightly over the back of her arm. She wasn't even sure he was aware that he was doing it. His gaze turned sober, his shoulders tense with concern.

"He wants to protect the integrity of the business." She understood the older man's reasons. Even the strongest companies could experience a downturn over rumors about a change in leadership.

"Yes." Ian's touch stilled as he met her gaze. "Even at the expense of his health. But you see why I am all the more concerned about protecting his legacy? Not for me, but for him?"

She understood about wanting approval. She'd craved it her whole life from her father and then, after his death, from her half siblings and the family she'd never gotten to know. But that had eluded her. Ian didn't have those kinds of concern, though. He knew his grandfather loved him.

"If keeping the company in the family was that important to him, don't you think he would alter the terms of the will?" She tipped her face to the sea breeze off the water, feeling off-kilter over having an intimate conversation with Ian at such close range. "Maybe your grandfather is more concerned with your happiness. I can't imagine he'd want you to marry someone just for the sake of keeping the business in the family."

"Malcolm McNeill was raised in a different time. He doesn't see the problem with choosing a bride for practical purposes." Ian released her but didn't move away, which in essence blocked her from leaving the cabana. "So I'm trying to see his reasoning in those terms. You and I make sense together, Lydia. We can help each other."

This would be so much easier if she didn't keep mixing up the past and the present, seeing her former lover in Ian instead of the hard, pragmatic man she knew him to be. Even last year, he'd put his grandfather's wishes before hers, so why should it surprise her that he would marry for the sake of his family? Yet no matter how hard she tried, she saw the man who made love to her in a waterfall at dawn. A man who'd shown her a level of pleasure in bed she'd never imagined possible.

A man who'd held her heart in his strong palm.

"I can't help you." Her words were soft, fragile things, not nearly as fierce as she would have liked.

"What could I do to make you say yes?" He corralled a flyaway strand of hair and smoothed it behind her ear. "Just name it."

He was offering her the chance to keep her matchmaking business and protect her identity from another scandal. He'd keep Vitaly Koslov at bay and give her a kind of respectability she'd never known as the daughter of a notorious tabloid diva. All of which would be very beneficial.

Now, he was even allowing her to dictate her terms.

She couldn't deny she was tempted. Especially now that she knew his motive wasn't payback for the matches she'd sent him last fall. She believed he was truly worried about his grandfather's health and fulfilling one of the old man's wishes.

"Separate rooms." The words came tumbling from her mouth before she'd really thought through all the ways this could go wrong. "Help with my matchmaking business if I need it." She remembered what Kinley had said about the McNeill family's access to A-list events that would be difficult to get into otherwise.

"I don't know a lot about matchmaking," he admitted. "I would have thought you and I were going to be great together."

Her heart squeezed tight, remembering that she'd thought the same thing until she'd discovered he was only using their relationship to fill the time until he found the right woman to marry. Now it seemed Ian didn't mind compromising his standards for a wife when he was in a hurry.

"Not that kind of help. I mean it might aid my work if I could use the McNeill name to meet more potential clients."

"Done." Ian didn't hesitate. "It's a deal then?"

A deal? For real? She must have lost her mind

for considering this. But it was only for twelve months, right?

"I would have one other condition." She swallowed hard, needing to be forthright with him if she was going to go through with this.

He stayed silent, which somehow swayed her more than a million words.

She found herself speaking slowly, weighing each thought, almost like dipping her toe in to test the waters. "I would expect you to honor what you said earlier about not using seduction as a weapon." Her voice did that high, breathy thing again, and she swallowed hard to make it go away. "While I acknowledge there is a pull between us, Ian, I need you to promise me you won't take advantage of that."

"On one condition." His voice lowered. His forehead tipped closer to hers.

Her heart pounded like it wanted to leap free of her chest.

"What?" She should have spelled out that he couldn't even get this close to her.

What had she been thinking?

"I get to kiss you on two occasions."

Kisses. Just kisses. But when had they ever been able to stop at just kisses?

She should protest. End this now. Let Vitaly Koslov sue her into bankruptcy for embarrassing his ballerina daughter by sending her a marriage-minded suitor to propose to her in front of the press.

Instead, Lydia breathed in the feel of having Ian this close to her. So close she caught a hint of his sandalwood aftershave that had occasionally clung to her skin after a night in his bed.

"When would those kisses happen?" Her eyes tracked his. "On what occasions?"

"Once on our wedding day. And once to seal the deal."

"As in...now?" She would not lick her lips even though her mouth went chalk-dry at the thought.

"Right now." His hand found the center of her back, his palm an electric warmth through the mesh fabric of her cover-up. "Do we have a deal, Lydia? One year together and I'll honor all of your terms."

Bad idea, bad idea, her brain chanted, as if to urge the words out of her mouth. But she could not forsake the women—the mothers—who needed her help. And selfishly, she could not put herself through another scandal.

She nodded her assent.

A wicked, masculine smile curved his lips.

"I'm so glad to hear it." His blue eyes glowed with a new heat in that moment of victory right before he lowered his mouth to hers.

* * *

If one kiss was all he got until their vows, Ian planned to make it count.

His hands cupped her waist just above the gentle curve of her hips. Her skin was warm through the thin mesh cover-up. She pressed closer, or maybe he did, the space between them shrinking until her breasts teased against his chest, the soft swell of sweet feminine flesh making him ache for a better feel of her.

Hunger for her roared down Ian's spine the moment their lips touched. The electric connection they'd always had sparked to flame, singeing his insides with a need to have her. Here. Now. He could lower the curtains on the cabana for privacy and ease her beautiful body down to the table. With no effort at all he could sweep aside that scrap of fabric that counted as a swimsuit and be deep inside her. He knew her body so well. Felt the answering heat in the breathless way she kissed him back, her fingernails clutching lightly at his shirt to keep him close.

Even now, she fit her body to his, her hips arching into him. Or maybe her legs felt as weak beneath her as his did and she was simply melting against him.

Yes.

He reached behind her, just above her head, to release the tie holding back one side of the cabana's front curtain. The fabric fell in a rush, cloaking them in shadows. Lydia levered back, blinking up at the change in the light. She focused on the fallen length of white fabric.

"What are you doing?" Her lips trembled. "Why?"

He couldn't take his eyes off her mouth.

"Giving us more privacy." He kissed her again, feeding on the plump softness until her lips parted.

He turned them both, pinning her to him with one hand at the small of her back while he flicked free the other side of the cabana curtain, letting it tumble to the ground and shield them completely from view of anyone else on the beach.

"A kiss." Her words whispered over his mouth in a soft sigh. "We said one kiss."

"We did." He bent to taste the skin just below her ear, feeling her pulse beat fast. "And see how well that turned out for both of us?"

"Ian." She fisted her hands tighter in his shirt for a moment, then edged back from him.

Wide-eyed in the newly dim interior of the closed cabana, she gazed up at him while the white curtains shifted gently in the breeze off the water. He listened to the waves roll in to keep his focus off the way she looked with her cover-up sliding off one shoulder and her lips swollen from his kiss.

He needed to be patient. To not push for more. It would be better when she came to him because she was ready to pick up where they left off. But damn. Keeping his hands off her right now when the air between them pulsed with want and heat proved a staggering test of restraint.

"Yes?" He wanted to trace the fullness of her lower lip. Memorize the feel of her.

"How fast is this going to happen? A marriage, I mean?"

She was talking about marriage? A surge of triumph pumped through him. This deal was all but done.

He held back his victory shout and kept his voice level. "I hope you're asking because you're looking forward to that next kiss as much as I am."

"I'm wondering how to handle us being on the same job in the same city. If we're supposed to look like a couple, and if that's okay while we're working together." She straightened her cover-up and took a step back from him.

He tugged the privacy curtain back into place on one side of the cabana, giving up on the idea of resurrecting their relationship with impromptu sex on the breakfast table.

Patience.

"I'll find a justice of the peace and see how quickly we can put in the paperwork." He would rest easier when he knew he was on track to meet the terms of his grandfather's will. The sooner they got married, the sooner that would happen.

His brother Quinn and his ballerina fiancée

were due to wed in two weeks. With any luck, Ian would already be wed to Lydia by then. Not that they needed to announce it until afterward.

"And you think we can stay on this job together as a couple, no emotions, no sex involved?" She seemed worried about that and he wondered why.

He'd never imagined her as overly concerned with finances. She was donating 100 percent of the money she made in her matchmaking business, after all. His friend Bentley's report had confirmed as much.

But then again, if she was so financially stable, he had to wonder about her accommodations at the old, worn-down Calypso Hotel.

"I will honor your wishes every step of the way. But to be certain, I'll speak to Jeremy today. And in the meantime, I have several vacant bedrooms at the suite at the Setai. I'll ask the concierge service to move your things." He sent out two text messages to arrange for her clothes to be delivered to the penthouse.

She'd said separate rooms. But she could hardly quibble when his suite was bigger than most private homes.

"There's one other thing. About the terms I mentioned?" She followed him out of the cabana across the sand, back toward his car. "I'd like to use your name to get into a party later this week. I think I'll get in more easily as your guest."

"I'll put you in touch with my assistant if we need an invitation. I'll go with you and we can debut our romantic relationship publicly." He withdrew his phone and sent a message to Mrs. Trager.

She paused near the Calypso.

"I'm parked this way." He pointed toward his vehicle in a spot up the street.

"But I should at least go shower and change."

"You can do both those things at my suite. For all we know we'll be able to marry by this afternoon." He took her hand and led her forward when she hesitated. "We might as well stick together."

"I can't believe we're really going through with this." She matched her steps to his, heading toward the BMW convertible. "Should we sign an agreement of some sort? I'd feel better if we had things in writing."

"Of course." He would ensure their terms were spelled out clearly. Put her at ease with the plan so she could relax and enjoy the benefits of marriage.

Because the next time they kissed, he planned to take his time reminding her how very rewarding the next twelve months together could be.

Six

Three whirlwind days later, shortly before noon, Lydia stood in front of a Dade County justice of the peace and signed the documents to become Ian's wife.

Privately, they'd already signed the papers spelling out the terms for separation in one year. She'd had a trusted attorney look over it to be sure she understood all aspects of the document and agreed the settlement was fair. Ian had added numerous financial benefits that she'd had stricken from the agreement since she wasn't marrying him for a cash prize, for crying out loud. They'd argued about it more than once, but in the end, he'd capitulated when she'd flat-out refused to sign under those terms.

Now, signing her name beside Ian's in the public register, Lydia clutched her flowers tighter as the simple ceremony got underway. They hadn't even forewarned their families. But though there was no fanfare, she wore an ivory silk cocktail dress that Ian had ordered for the occasion. He'd insisted it was his tailor's idea since her dress matched the accessories on his charcoal silk suit. And she had to admit the lines of the sheath gown with its wide-set straps and square neck were pretty without shouting "bridal" when they'd walked into the courthouse.

So she watched the petals of the peach-colored lilies tremble in her bouquet while the justice of the peace made their temporary marriage official. She'd barely had time to think since agreeing to all this, from moving into the luxury penthouse suite of Ian's hotel to explaining her upcoming nuptials to Kinley and doing her job for the Foxfire after Ian had officially disclosed their relationship to Jeremy Singer. Since that last heated kiss on the beach, Ian hadn't pressed for further physical intimacy, which didn't surprise her since they'd agreed she would set the pace.

And yet, had he thought about those electric moments in the cabana as often as she had? Knowing that another kiss awaited them today—their wedding day—only added to the butterflies in her stomach as the judge made their marriage official. This time, however, things wouldn't spiral out of control the way they had at the beach. For one thing, she was prepared this time.

For another, there were witnesses, for crying out loud. Strangers, perhaps, but legal witnesses nevertheless.

As Lydia peered up into Ian's blue eyes and the rest of the world seemed to disappear, she acknowledged that he had the power to make her completely forget herself. It was why she'd need to be very careful during the next twelve months or she would lose her heart to him all over again. Because no matter how much her body responded to the chemistry they generated, her head understood that Ian would always put the McNeills—the family and the business bearing their name—before her.

Ian was impeccably dressed in a custom-tailored H. Huntsman two-button gray silk suit, a white shirt with an ivory silk tie and a pocket square that took the outfit to another level of formal. She had to admit his tailor was correct in suggesting the outfits—their wedding photo snapped by the secretary out front was bound to be beautiful. For a wistful moment, Lydia wished she had Kinley with her to share what was normally a momentous occasion in a woman's life. But in the end, she'd thought it was best to simply keep the nuptials quiet until the marriage was a *fait accompli* since Lydia's mother would have been the first to insinuate herself into the media coverage.

"And now for the presentation of the rings," the justice of the peace announced, startling Lydia from her reverie and inducing a moment of panic.

Ian had said he'd take care of that. Had he remembered?

But he was already producing platinum bands. One was plain and masculine with some kind of etching. The other had a square yellow diamond in a cushion-cut setting that made her gasp out loud. The clerk continued, prompting them to repeat after him the standard vows from the simplest ceremony offered. Lydia repeated the words, hoping she wasn't making a colossal mistake, as she slid Ian's ring onto his finger and accepted the gorgeous canary sparkler on her own hand.

"I now declare you man and wife," the justice of the peace intoned, closing the black leather book he read from and shuffling it to one side of the polished oak desk behind him. "You may kiss your bride."

Lydia couldn't have said which idea provided the greater shock to her system. That she was now Ian's wife? Or that his lips were about to covers hers again?

She saw the glow of possessive fire in her groom's eyes—or maybe she just felt the answering fire in her blood. Either way, her heart rate increased to double-time and the silk bodice of her gown seemed to shrink, cutting off her air as she held her breath for a suspended moment.

When Ian dipped closer, however, he merely brushed his lips along her cheek and whispered in her ear.

"I'm banking the real kiss for later," he promised, the deep timbre of his voice smoking over her skin and calling to mind heated scenarios she felt sure no proper bride would be dreaming about at the altar.

Or, in this case, at the courthouse desk.

Off-kilter from that whispered vow and her new marital status, Lydia smiled woodenly for another photo as Ian finished their business and took copies of their paperwork. They didn't speak again until they left the courtroom and their words wouldn't be overheard.

"Congratulations, Mrs. McNeill," Ian told her as he took her hand and led her from the building out into the heat of a Miami afternoon.

They'd traveled inland and north of the city for the courthouse visit, but Lydia hadn't paid much attention to their surroundings that morning when they'd parked the car. She'd been too nervous. Now she felt even more on edge thinking about Ian's plan to bank that kiss.

She lowered her nose to the bouquet of lilies

and roses and inhaled the fresh fragrance to soothe her nerves.

"Congratulations to us both. We've fooled the world into thinking we are in love for the sake of our personal objectives." She hadn't meant to taint the day with the bitterness she felt since it would be easier to simply coast along like none of this was getting to her.

But something about the dress and the beautiful diamond now on her hand—all the trappings of a real wedding—had gotten under her skin.

"We've merely set aside our differences to help one another." He waved over a dark luxury SUV that was not the vehicle they'd arrived in. "Let's celebrate the occasion, shall we?"

Lydia's silk kitten heels skidded on the pavement as she halted. Ian slowed his step to take her elbow. Steady her.

"What do you mean?" She kept her eye on the SUV as it pulled up to the curb beside them, the tinted windows dark enough to prevent her from seeing inside. "I have an online meeting with an overseas supplier this afternoon."

She needed to regain her equilibrium. Work would help with that.

"I remember." Ian gave a nod toward the SUV and at his signal, a liveried driver stepped from the vehicle. "I've got a conference room prepared for you. I was hoping to sit in on some of it since

I think this group has some architectural salvage pieces that could be incorporated into the court-yard design."

The driver opened the rear door of the SUV, revealing champagne-colored bucket seats as a blast of air-conditioning cooled Lydia's skin. A passing vehicle honked its horn at them as someone shouted "Congratulations, newlyweds!"

"You see?" Ian's hand slid around her waist to nudge her gently forward. "Everyone else wants us to seize the day. You can work for two hours while we are in the air and by the time you're done we'll be almost ready to land. Tonight, we can toast our marriage while the sun sets over the Pacific."

She didn't budge. The last time she'd been in the Pacific with him, she'd ended up pregnant.

"You know I wouldn't want to go back there—"

"Of course." He shook his head, lowering his voice for her ears only. "I wouldn't take you to Ran-giroa. But we can be in Costa Rica in a couple of hours. We could have a decadent dinner overlook-ing the water, then return in the morning."

Lydia wondered far more about what could hap-pen in the time *between* that decadent dinner and the flight home in the morning. Yet she was re-lieved to know Ian hadn't tried to resurrect the magic of last spring in the Polynesian islands when she'd fallen head over heels. Too many memories in that part of the world.

"I was not expecting anything like this. I don't have anything packed." She should probably have just said no outright. But the gesture was thoughtful even if it was more over-the-top than something she would have chosen.

"Taken care of. And if we are going to spend a year in close proximity, I think it would benefit us to try and find our footing as friends." He nodded at the driver again, chasing the attendant back to the front of the vehicle without a word.

"Friends." She tested the idea, unable to imagine such a tepid term for the relationship they'd once shared. But since that was in the past, perhaps he had a point. "This seems highly romantic for friendship."

"We just wed, Lydia. The illusion of a quick honeymoon will only cement our story for the rest of the world—our families included."

"So it's also for show." She nodded thoughtfully. She knew Ian would honor their agreement. There would be separate rooms. He would let her make the next move. She trusted in this implicitly because she knew his sense of honor.

It was that damnable kiss that had her rattled.

"And I think you'll enjoy being out of town when the news breaks about our nuptials," he reminded her.

Oddly, that won her over more than anything else he might have said. The thought of being in the papers—for any reason—made her skin crawl after growing up with her attention-seeking mother. As a bonus, she would have every reason in the world to ignore calls from her mom about her marriage for a little while longer.

"Deal." Lydia slid onto her seat inside the SUV and told herself the time together could be put to good use anyhow. She would speak to him about setting boundaries and house rules for living together over the next year once they settled into dinner.

Or, better yet, she would keep that topic for their *after*-dinner conversation. Because as the SUV whisked them away toward the nearest private airport, she knew she needed to figure out a way to fill that mysterious void of time between their meal and the return flight home.

Ian might be entitled to one more kiss, but she planned to make certain it didn't lead to a wedding night.

"I thought you weren't concerned with the terms of Gramps's will." Cameron McNeill scolded during a teleconference Ian was holding on board the chartered Gulfstream currently flying Lydia and him to Costa Rica for the night.

Ian had been sitting in the jet's small conference room with Lydia when his phone went berserk with repeated texts from both his brothers. Excusing himself from the online meeting with the overseas supplier to let Lydia handle it, Ian had taken a seat in the lounge and put his feet up before he dialed Quinn's office in New York, hoping to speak to his older—more coolheaded—sibling first.

But apparently Quinn only found out about the secret wedding because Cameron had barged into his office with an eight-by-ten printer blow-up of the photo taken at the Dade County clerk's office. Who leaked the information was anyone's guess since neither Ian nor Lydia was particularly well-known outside their social and professional circles, but clearly someone had keyed in on the McNeill name and publicized Ian's hasty marriage. The article Cameron had found was on a New York gossip blog, but the story was making the rounds in other places, fueled in part—Ian would guess—by how knockout beautiful Lydia looked in that ivory gown. She had a Mona Lisa smile in the photo, but there was something unmistakably mischievous in her bright green eyes.

No wonder the tabloids couldn't post the story fast enough.

"I didn't marry her just because of the will," Ian argued. "We had a prior relationship. Although I will admit, our grandfather's heart attack gave his terms a new sense of urgency."

Both his brothers were in Quinn's office in the Financial District back in New York. Quinn rested one hip on the window seat with a view of midtown behind him while Cameron paced the large office with the restless energy of a caged animal. Tall and rangy, he almost didn't fit in the frame captured by the webcam as he stalked back and forth in front of the antique bookshelves. Ian adjusted the angle on the fold-down screen above his seat to cut the glare from a nearby window as the plane began its descent.

He'd far rather be staring at his bride right now, but Lydia sat behind a partition in a separate section of the plane intended for teleconferencing on a big screen.

"You both told me Gramps was bluffing," Cameron reminded them. "You said he would back off on this. And now Ian tied the knot in secret and Quinn's getting married in two weeks." Cameron flung himself into the leather chair behind Quinn's oversize desk, wheeling the seat back a few feet. "I'm beginning to think it's you two who are bluffing."

"Our point, Cameron," Quinn interjected, loosening his gray silk tie, "was that you shouldn't marry for Gramps's sake. If you meet the right woman, that's one thing." He turned toward the camera—and Ian. "And I'm assuming this was a serious relationship for Ian to make him think of marrying."

Talking down Cameron's bluster was far easier

than working his way around Quinn's canny gaze. The oldest of the three, Quinn had taken on the parenting role early when their mother divorced their father and the three McNeill sons split the year between the two of them. In Rio, with their mother, they were well supervised. The rest of the time, if their thrill-seeking, globe-trotting father, Liam, was in charge, Quinn proved a more reliable guardian for the three of them.

"Of course." Ian's reasons for marrying Lydia were complex enough that he wasn't entirely certain he could pick through them all himself. But he regretted walking out of her life without a fight last spring. He should have stayed. Should have been there for her when she miscarried their child. Now? He might have torched the old feelings for her, but he could damn well build on what they'd had before. He was comfortable with a marriage built on a legal foundation. He understood the terms and knew what was expected—unlike last time when he'd fallen too far too fast.

When both Quinn and Cameron stared at him expectantly, Ian realized he needed to offer up some kind of explanation. Not easy to do when he'd agreed not to reveal the secret of Mallory West.

"Lydia and I met last year when I was supervising the hotel project in Rangiroa." He clicked on his seat belt when he heard the chime overhead from the pilot and saw the sign go on. His gaze went to the conference room door, but it was still closed so Lydia must be buckling in for the descent in there. "We had a strong connection, but we wanted to see if it was because we met in a tropical paradise or if the bond could withstand the real world. Turns out, we're very good for each other."

Quinn frowned. Cameron's eyes widened.

"You dated for a year without telling anyone about her?" Cam asked, spearing his fingers through his dark hair.

"No." Ian should have thought through his response more before having this conversation but he wanted it done, and after the constant texts, he'd realized the McNeills weren't going to let a secret wedding stand without an inquisition. "We had our ups and downs, but we reconnected on the South Beach project and felt drawn to be together. We agreed we didn't want to detract from Quinn and Sofia's wedding so we thought we'd marry quietly. It didn't occur to me that filing for a license would flag any media interest."

"Wrong on that count, dude." Cameron reached for the eight-by-ten photo of the courthouse wedding and waved it. "This sucker was making the rounds half an hour after you did the deal."

Ian gritted his teeth. "Quinn, please extend my apologies to Sofia if my awkward timing for the marriage upset her. We hoped to wait until after your wedding to announce ours. But if that's all, gentleman, I'm about ten minutes away from touching down in Costa Rica for my honeymoon."

"Sofia doesn't mind sharing the spotlight as a bride, only as a ballerina." The grin on Quinn's face was a new expression that they'd only started to see when the New York City Ballet dancer had entered his life.

Sometimes it still took Ian a second to reconcile that expression with his ever-serious older brother. He envied their complete devotion to one another. A kind of happiness Ian knew he'd never find in his temporary contract marriage.

There would be other rewards, however. For both of them.

Cameron elbowed Quinn. "Tell him why we really called, man."

Instantly on alert, Ian straightened, the fine leather in the chair squeaking as he moved.

"Is it Gramps? Is he okay?" He'd been worried about Malcolm McNeill's transition from Shanghai to New York, a trip that had been delayed twice because of his doctor's concerns and the need to travel with good medical equipment.

"He's fine," Quinn assured him. "But he contacted us today after your wedding photo circulated online. He wants to meet with all of us."

Ian's gut knotted. Tightened. "Of course. How soon?"

"No immediate rush. He wouldn't want to disrupt the honeymoon." Quinn rose from his spot at the window ledge and flipped a page on the desk calendar. "Three days from now, maybe? I'll be in New York then and so will Cam, right?" He glanced up at their youngest brother.

"Sure thing," Cam answered as the plane broke through the cloud cover and the Costa Rican mountains became visible in a wavy carpet of dark green below.

"I'll be there." Ian's honeymoon would be over by then. "Any idea what he wants?"

"No." Quinn shook his head, brow furrowed. "But I would bring Lydia with you. She's part of the family now."

Ian nodded as he disconnected the call, hating the hollow feeling in his chest. He'd had good reasons for this marriage, but they weren't anything his grandfather was going to understand or approve. Even now, his new wife tended to business just on the other side of that partition. He couldn't hear her conversation, but he knew she would be bargaining for the best price on the decor and artwork she hoped to secure for the Foxfire. But soon, they would be alone and they could figure out what this marriage meant for their future.

His arrangement with Lydia was strictly between the two of them. She understood what was at stake and so did he. No complicated emotions meant they wouldn't crash and burn like they had last year. As for her other terms?

A McNeill knew that everything was open for negotiation. And he still had one kiss to bargain with.

Seven

Mrs. Lydia McNeill.

Seated inside her dressing room at their private villa in Costa Rica late that afternoon, Lydia read the engraved luggage tag on the buttery leather suitcase tucked under a bamboo shelf of the walk-in closet off the bathroom of her suite.

None of this felt real. Not the suite at the Honeymoon House. Not the flight on a Gulfstream jet that she'd boarded with only a few minutes' notice. And certainly not her new name.

Her eyes wandered over the wardrobe selections some unnamed staffer of Ian's had chosen for her. There was a silk tropical print maxi dress with coral-colored hibiscus flowers on a white background. A teal-colored pair of gauzy palazzo pants with a white sequined crepe halter top. A silver evening gown that looked like something a fairy princess would wear with gossamer-thin layers of vaguely iridescent fabric. Designer everything, of course. There were other clothes stacked neatly on the bamboo shelves, as well. Italian-made underthings. A nightgown so soft and sheer it was perfect for a bride with its combination of innocence and sensuality.

Except she wasn't a bride in the real sense. And she would not be putting that gorgeous nightdress on her body tonight.

"Lydia?" Ian called from the other side of the bathroom door. "Can I get you anything?"

Her stomach did a fluttery flip at the sound of his voice so close in this piece of paradise. No doubt he wanted to make sure the clothes fit before the dinner they would share on the open-air patio. He'd seemed pleased to show her their accommodations for the night, stressing the way the separate bedrooms fit her requirements but also gave them a chance to celebrate a new peace between them.

Except she didn't feel one bit peaceful about this marriage. If anything, the tropical retreat on the country's western coast only emphasized all the ways today fell short of what she'd once hoped to share with him. If not for the need to hide the true identity of Mallory West, she never would have said yes to this arrangement. But she needed to protect her matchmaking business and the important income it gave to a cause that meant so much to her, to women who inspired her with their strength and determination to be good mothers no matter what obstacles life handed them. Her mother had afforded parenthood by making herself and her daughter tabloid spectacles. Worse, she'd put her energy into fueling that drama rather than showing up at science fairs or even Lydia's high school graduation, which had unfortunately coincided with a face-lift.

Small wonder Lydia felt called to champion single moms who genuinely adored motherhood.

"No. I'll be out in a moment," she called, forcing herself to her feet. The dressing area was as luxe as some women's living rooms with a comfortable leather chair, plenty of mirrors and soft ambient lighting. But she could hardly afford to languish here, staring at her married name on a luggage tag.

Pulling on the silk maxi dress, Lydia let the fabric fall over the soft, imported lace slip that was too beautiful not to wear. She'd never spend her hard-earned dollars as a decorator on something so extravagant, but a woman would have to be blind not to appreciate the careful stitchwork that went into such a delicate design.

"There's no rush. The sun set won't set for another half hour," he called. After a moment, Lydia could hear the sound of his footsteps as he retreated deeper into the resort villa.

Leaving her to remember how many sunsets they'd watched together last spring when they'd been falling in love.

Twelve.

She'd marked them on a calendar, because that was the kind of silly nonsense young women indulged in when they fell in love. They drew hearts around meaningful days in a date book and scribbled effusive prose punctuated with too many exclamation marks in diaries. Lydia had been guilty on all counts.

Emerging from the dressing area, she stepped into her bedroom where she'd left all the windows open to the fresh air. A white-faced capuchin monkey sat on the low stone wall behind her hammock, munching on a piece of mango. Beyond the terrace, she could see the path down to the ocean, hear the gentle rush of waves to the sand.

Any other time, she would have loved an impromptu trip like this to an exotic destination. Travel was her favorite thing about her job since she couldn't afford it otherwise. But tonight, she was getting ready to face her new husband over the dinner table, and that made her too nervous to fully enjoy the surroundings.

"Wish me luck," she called to the monkey before it hopped off the wall and into the pink glow of the coming sunset.

Then, leaving her bedroom, she climbed the stairs to the third story of their private villa and the open-air deck where a local restaurant had set up the catered meal.

"You look incredible." Ian greeted her near the outdoor stairs, offering his arm to escort her past the lone table in the middle of the wooden deck overlooking the ocean. "I hope you found the clothing options as appealing as I do."

His blue eyes never left hers as he spoke, yet her whole body responded to his words, a tingling sensation skipping along her skin. She couldn't help but notice how handsome he looked in a dark suit with a white linen shirt open at the neck. Formal, but with a touch of the reprobate about him.

And now he was her husband.

"Thank you." Clearing her throat, she thought it better not to linger on how well Ian McNeill wore a suit. "The whole place is beautiful." She gestured to the view overlooking the water, the elegant table for two set with a crisp white cloth and laden with silver dishes, bright tropical flowers in vases and seven wax tapers flickering in a candelabra. "I thought it was nice of your local chef to text us his menu suggestions beforehand."

She'd received a message from the chef on the plane, offering a selection of dishes made from the freshest ingredients his culinary staff obtained that morning.

"Were you brave enough to order the grilled octopus he recommended?" Ian teased, drawing her to the edge of the deck to watch the pink sun slip lower on the horizon. His hand lingered at her waist even after they reached the wooden railing, his fingers separated from her skin by the thinnest silk.

Her heartbeat sped faster and she concentrated on the fragrant angel's trumpet flowers spilling over the railing at their feet, sending their heady perfume into the air to mingle with the salty brine of the ocean. Monkeys and birds called to one another as they hastened to their homes before dark fell. Better to think about monkeys and birds than the way Ian's touch affected her.

"I went with the Thai coconut shrimp and pineapple. The preparation sounded suitably tropical." The breeze blew a strand of hair across her chin.

Before she could fix it, Ian reached to skim it aside and tuck it behind one ear, his touch slow and warm. Deliberate.

Oh. So. Inviting.

"There's fresh mango salsa if you're ready for hors d'oeuvres." His voice rumbled low, vibrating along her sensitive skin. "Are you hungry, Lydia?"

Her gaze flashed up to his. Did he know how hard she struggled with the temptation he presented? Was he teasing her again?

But his blue eyes appeared concerned, not intent on seduction. Perhaps she shouldn't rush to judge him.

"I wouldn't mind a drink while the sun sets." Her mouth was dry and her heart felt more than a little bruised to undergo the trappings of marriage without the feelings that should go along with it. "Maybe we should have our toast now."

"Certainly." He excused himself to pour the champagne from a bucket chilling on a stand near their table. "I hope you don't mind, but we'll be serving ourselves tonight. The honeymoon suite service is…discreet in that way."

"Of course." She tensed, crossing her arms. "That way, if we decide we have to tear each other's clothes off before dessert, we'll have complete privacy to do so."

Ian finished pouring the champagne, but she could see his shoulders stiffen underneath the impeccably tailored suit jacket.

"I guess we would. But since you've been very clear about your expectations in this marriage, I realize that's not going to happen tonight." He stalked toward her, a champagne flute in each hand. "And that's another reason I thought it would be best for the waitstaff not to be around. I want to protect your privacy and respect your wishes about all things."

Somehow that consideration made her heart beat

faster still. The sea breeze tickled the silk of her dress against her thighs and toyed with the spaghetti straps on her shoulders, a phantom lover's touch. She needed a dose of reality back in this faux honeymoon.

"You say that." She tugged the flute from his hands with a bit more force than necessary, her emotions getting the better of her as a few bubbles slid over the side of the glass. "And yet you persist in pretending that this is a real marriage with a flight to Costa Rica and a sunset meal in a villa called the Honeymoon House. I can't help but feel the weight of very different expectations."

"Lydia." He set his glass on the railing then guided hers there, too. "We need to present the world with a believable marriage or our agreement isn't worth anything." He folded both of her hands in his, turning her to face him. "I spoke to my brothers on the flight here and they informed me that news of our nuptials has already been leaked. Believe me when I tell you, the world is watching what happens next."

"Leaked?" She tried to imagine how that could happen. "Why? Who would care about our marriage?" Panic tightened in her chest as she thought of all the horrible ways the tabloids could ratchet up interest in a story. She'd been the object of media interest far too often in her life. "What are they saying?"

"Only that we married. Someone in the district court offices must have leaked the news directly since my brothers had a copy of the wedding photo within thirty minutes of the ceremony."

"If they aren't saying anything ugly yet, they will soon." She needed to sit. Or maybe walk. She didn't know what she needed, but she felt all the makings of a full-blown panic attack coming on. "Excuse me."

Pulling away from his touch, she paced the deck.

"There is nothing ugly to say," Ian assured her, watching her progress but not following her, which she appreciated.

"Then they make something up. That's how the tabloids sell their sordid work." She recalled old headlines from her past—stories about her mother. Stories about her. "Did you know there was a whole year where the media sold papers on the idea that my mother was part of a religious cult that cast a spell on my father?" They'd taken a laughable photo of her mother in a Halloween costume and used it for weeks on end. "Then, there was a whole other year where they used zoom lenses to snap photos of her stomach to analyze it for a baby bump. And one extremely hellish year when *I* was photographed and accused of having a baby bump. At sixteen."

She didn't mention the stories that suggested her mother had pimped her out to rich men for a fat payday. Or the fact that she'd been treated for an eating disorder after being accused of looking pregnant as a vulnerable teenager.

Feeling a wealth of old resentment threaten to wash over her like a rogue wave, Lydia took the wooden stairs leading away from the third-floor deck all the way down to the beach. Vaguely, she heard Ian call out to her, and his footsteps as he followed her. She didn't stop, though. She couldn't get enough air into her lungs no matter how deeply she breathed. Kicking off her jeweled sandals, she let her toes sink into the powdery sand as she hurried down to the water's edge.

By the time Ian reached her side, she had the hem of her long silk maxi dress in one hand, the fabric hiked up to her knees so she could stand in the rolling surf. The warm water soothed her, lapping gently along her calves and beading up on her skin slick with the coconut oil lotion supplied as a resort amenity. Somehow the feel of the water against her skin took her heart rate down a notch, and she tipped her face into the soft sea breeze.

Ian removed his socks and shoes at the water's edge, preparing to join her. She thought about telling him not to bother—that she was okay—but then she wondered why she needed to pretend she was fine when she so often wasn't.

She'd denied herself comfort in life many times out of the need to look like she had her life together and a deep-seated desire to avoid scandal. But no matter what she did, she was a favorite target of the tabloid media. She could live the most pristine, blameless life possible and they'd still find some way to make a tawdry tale out of her.

And right now, as she watched Ian stride toward her with his broad shoulders that looked like they could take on the problems of the world, she had to wonder why she kept denying herself pleasure for the sake of a good reputation she would never achieve.

Ian McNeill was her husband. He was the most generous, amazing lover she'd ever had. And he'd made it very clear that he still wanted her.

As long as she could separate pleasure from a deep emotional commitment, couldn't she at least indulge herself for a little while?

Ian had almost reached Lydia's side when she sent him a look that sizzled over him like a lover's tongue.

The sensation was so tangible he had to halt his forward progress through the shallow surf. No way had he read her expression correctly. He was mixing up his own emotions with hers—seeing what he wanted to see in her bright green eyes. His heart slugged harder in his chest, urging him toward her, while he fought the need with all his might.

She'd just shared some hurtful memories he

never knew about, so no way in hell was she thinking what he was thinking.

Get it together.

"Lydia." He forced an even tone into his voice, reminding himself that good men didn't confuse compassion with sex. "I'm so sorry you went through that as a teen."

He reached for her, cupping her cheek in one hand even as he maintained a bit of space between them. Her eyes slid closed at his touch, her cheek tilting into his palm in a way that urged him to give more physical comfort.

Reigniting the war within.

Gritting his teeth against all the ways he wanted to surround her body with his—protect her, pleasure her—Ian shifted closer to slide an arm around her waist. He drew her against him, fitting her to his side, resting his cheek on top of her silky hair. The scent of coconut drifted up from her skin. His mouth watered.

"I promise you," he assured her, stroking along the soft skin of her upper arm while he stared out to sea, "if anyone dares to initiate a story about you that isn't true, I will sue their company into bankruptcy."

"They will say I married you for money." She pulled back to look him in the eye. "The same way my mother pursued my father."

"We both know nothing could be further from

the truth." He'd tried to include a financial settlement in their contract, but she'd refused. Had she done so because she anticipated that kind of negative press?

"Your family will have their doubts about my intentions in this marriage. As will all of Manhattan. I received a famously small settlement from my father upon his death." She knotted the silk of her skirt at one knee so she didn't need to hold on to the fabric to keep it out of the water. "There will be questions about my motives for marrying you and the press speculation will only fuel the fire."

He'd seen that trick with a skirt hem in Rangiroa a few times, and he liked this side of her that was a little messier.

"My family has faith in my judgment." He'd already told them to stand down where she was concerned. "And that means they will trust you."

When she didn't answer right away, he noticed that she was staring out at the horizon where the sun was sliding the rest of the way into the sea. She'd told him once that she liked to make a wish on it before it disappeared.

"I wish *you* could trust me to make you happy for the next twelve months." He got the words out just before the final glowing orange arc vanished.

The sky glowed pink and purple in the aftermath, the ocean reflecting the colors in watery ripples while a heron and a pair of white ibis flew overhead.

"I don't think that's such a good thing to wish for." She turned to face him, her exposed skin reflecting the sunset hues.

"No?"

"No," she told him flatly. "Investing too much in this marriage will only make things all the more complicated when our year together is done." She folded her arms across her chest and stared down into the water where they stood. "We both need to remember this is a business arrangement. Nothing more."

"One thing doesn't have to preclude the other, does it?" He turned his attention to her arm, where the strap of her dress flirted with the edge of her shoulder. "We can be happy and respect the business arrangement, too."

Maybe this time together would help cure him of his preoccupation with her. He'd barely dated since they'd split.

"I've been thinking about that." She glanced down at the water where the gentle swell of the tide lapped at her ankles. She lifted one foot and skimmed it over the surface in a slow arc in front of her. "About the benefits of marriage."

His throat dried up. He stayed very still to keep from touching her the way he wanted to, convincing her with his hands and his mouth how *bene-*

ficial this relationship could be for both of them. He'd promised her she could set the pace with any kind of physical relationship and he wouldn't earn her trust anytime soon if he took that power out of her hands.

But the temptation to draw her into the water—into his arms—was so strong he could barely breathe.

"Like Costa Rican vacations?" He tried for a light tone but failed, his whole body fueled with a biological imperative to take his bride to his bed.

"This is definitely a treat." She quit her game of drawing her toes through the water, turning to face him in air that felt suddenly too still. "But I was thinking more along the lines of how—" she bit her lip for a second before pressing on "—*satisfying* we both found our previous relationship."

Blood pounded through his temples for a split second before surging south.

"Meaning you're reconsidering the idea of separate bedrooms?" He kept his eyes on hers in the growing dimness despite the flickering tiki torches dotting the sand near Honeymoon House. "We need to be very clear about this point, Lydia, since it's your move next."

During the heavy beat of silence that followed, an owl hooted from a tree nearby. In the distance, Ian spied a party boat on the waves, the music cranked high as the vessel sped through the dark water.

"It occurs to me that no matter how hard I've tried to live beyond reproach, I'm always going to be a target for the tabloids. In their eyes, my mother was a gold digger who duped my father into getting her pregnant. And I'm the bait she used to ensure she got her payoff." Lydia shrugged and the spaghetti strap that had been teetering on the edge of her shoulder gave up the ghost, sliding down her arm. "Why should I create some exaggerated facade of respectability when I'll forever be a tabloid story waiting to happen?"

He dragged his gaze from her bare shoulder and the delicate curve of her neck. "You make it sound like being with me compromises your reputation."

"No. I only mean that I have to stop worrying about what other people think of me and find what happiness I can. Because no matter what I do or how careful I am, I will be a magnet for rumors."

He sifted through her words. Put them in the context of the one question that burned brightest in his brain as the stars began to dot the sky above them.

"You want to find happiness." This seemed highly relevant. "And you agree that there were *satisfying* aspects of our relationship before things fell apart." Heat burned over him despite the fact that he stood ankle-deep in the Pacific. He wanted a taste of her more than he wanted his next breath as the tropical air blanketed his skin with sultry touches.

"Correct." She kept her arms clenched around herself, but there was no mistaking the challenging tilt of her chin. The throaty edge in her voice.

He waded an inch closer. Their bodies weren't touching. But the water swirled between them in circles that seemed to connect them anyway.

"Can I assume that you're open to revisiting those satisfying aspects?" He wouldn't have to use his kiss as a bargaining tool to woo her into his bed tonight.

"I'm starting to think it would be foolish to deny ourselves." Her words were breathless, a barely there sound that caressed his ears.

"I couldn't agree more." He waited for her touch. Watched for it.

Even the cries of birds and monkeys seemed to quiet in the still moment of her decision.

"It's my wedding night," she informed him, her voice picking up strength and volume. "I don't need to sleep alone."

"Not when I want you in my bed for days on end," he assured her, only too happy to describe exactly how thoroughly he would pleasure her if given the opportunity to touch her tonight. "Although I will be very disappointed if we are sleeping."

Despite the growing dark, he could see the convulsive movement of her throat as she swallowed. Licked her lips.

"Ian?"

"Mmm?"

"I think I'd like that kiss now."

Eight

A year ago, they would have fallen on each other with the ravenous hunger of lovers who need to be touching all the time.

Truth be told, she was so ready for his kiss, she felt more than a little ravenous now as they stood in the surf outside Honeymoon House.

But their relationship was much different now. Careful. Tenuous. And—she still couldn't believe it—they were married. Maybe that's why Ian took his time closing the distance between them. Instead of taking her in his arms, he stroked along her bare shoulder where one strap of her gown had fallen away. She hadn't realized how cool her skin was from standing in the water until she felt the warmth of his hand when he made contact. His callus-roughened palms reminded her he wasn't the kind of developer who simply drew plans, although he was talented enough to design his own buildings.

No. She'd seen Ian McNeill clamber up ladders and take a crowbar to stubborn wall supports himself, never afraid of getting his hands dirty on a job site. She liked that his millions hadn't robbed him of the ability to walk among the workmen or appreciate the less glamorous aspects of actual physical construction.

"Are you cold?" he asked, perhaps feeling the difference in their skin temperatures, and yet still he didn't kiss her in spite of her request. He held back, even as the fire in his eyes broadcast how much he wanted her.

"I'm not chilly at all. Thank you, though." She was plenty hot on the inside; in fact, she was anticipating that kiss, aching for him to take her lips. To take her. "I like being outside." She could breathe deeply out here without feeling suffocated by all the expectations weighing her down back home. Without the scandal rocking her world again.

"You're trembling," he observed softly, his other hand coming between them to skim a knuckle along her lower lip, drawing out the moment.

Lydia nipped it to put an end to that line of conversation since she was overwhelmed by her feelings for him. *Sensual feelings*, she told herself. *Nothing deeper*. The trembling didn't have a thing to do with romantic notions about the relationship she was undertaking again.

Finally—*thank goodness*—Ian cupped her face and tipped her chin up, perhaps to see her better in the moonlight. The glow of the tiki torches on the beach and dotting the railing of the deck on the third floor of Honeymoon House didn't give off enough light to see each other well now that the sun had set.

The look in his eyes sent of a flash fire along her skin. Brooding and intense, he stared at her as if she were a complicated puzzle he'd rather devour than solve. So when his kiss came, she was surprised by its devastating gentleness. His soft, full lips covered hers, coaxing them apart to taste and explore.

Sighing into him, she gave herself up to the wholly masculine feel of his strong arms wrapped around her. The hint of sandalwood on his skin unleashed a torrent of fiery memories. Stripping each other's clothes off in a hotel dining room because they couldn't wait to get to the bedroom. Ian slipping her swimsuit aside to pleasure her behind an island waterfall where no one could see them. Her hoarse shouts of fulfillment when he'd demonstrated a deftness with his tongue that had been her undoing, not just once, but many, many times.

Past and present mingling, Lydia pressed her body to all that hard, masculine heat, wanting to lose herself in him. In pleasure. No holding back. She wanted those memories to be reality now. The good memories. Not the aftermath of lies and deceit.

She worked the buttons of his linen dress shirt, hastily unfastening each one to splay greedy hands over his sculpted chest and abs. The moonlight shone down on his bronzed skin, making her greedy to see more of him. All of him.

"I want to take you inside." He captured her questing fingers, stilling her hungry explorations before he kissed the fingertips, one at a time. "I need to see you."

With a jerky nod, she agreed, even though she could have gladly pulled *An Affair to Remember* moment and wrestled him to the beach to make love in the surf.

Together, they hurried out of the water. He scooped up both pairs of shoes and set them on the first stair leading to the villa. She followed him barefoot up the wooden steps and onto the cool stone patio of the first floor. Here, the light from the small gas torches set at intervals in the stone railing cast plenty of light on them as he led her toward the outdoor shower.

And while she would have also pulled her dress off then and there, Ian turned on the shower spray at foot level just long enough to rinse the beach sand from their toes. She unfastened the knot she'd put in her dress hem to hold it up, letting the silk fall back around her calves while he shut off the nozzle.

She eyed his strong back as he straightened, the ripple of muscles evident through the thin, pale linen of his shirt.

"Damn, Lydia, you're killing me when you look at me like that."

Ian tugged her closer with one hand. Caught openly ogling him, she felt her cheeks heat and was glad for the rosy glow of the torchlight.

"I'm sure I don't know what you mean," she told him archly, turning to head up the stairs since both bedrooms were situated on the second floor.

"What I'd like to know—" he palmed the small of her back, shadowing her movements as his voice overwhelmed her senses "—is what you're thinking about when you look at me that way."

"Probably something really benign," she lied, teasing him only because she knew there would be an end to both their torments soon. "Like what you'll think of the outdoor rugs I chose for the Fox-fire courtyard."

She paused in the hallway between the two bedrooms, unsure which way to go. The villa was exposed to the Costa Rican elements on three sides and they'd left all the retractable windows open to savor the mild weather. She could see into his bedroom where a king-size platform bed covered in a black duvet and batik-patterned pillows was illuminated only by the flickering outdoor torches of the master suite's deck.

"Rugs? Not even close," he taunted lightly as he steered her toward his bedroom and the small shelter it offered from the thick, jungle-like branches that brushed against the open half walls. "I'll bet you were thinking about how much you wanted our clothes off."

He turned her to face him and her heart raced a crazy staccato beat as her gaze fell to his bare chest where she'd already undone half the buttons on his shirt.

"If we're being totally honest—" she hooked her finger into the gap of the soft linen and wrangled another button free, her knuckle grazing the warmth of those beautifully chiseled abs "—I was far more fixated on getting your clothes off than my own."

"That can be arranged." He stood in shadow, his back to the glow of torchlight while he shrugged out of the shirt, letting the expensive material float to the floor behind him. "I'll gladly do what it takes to put that gleam in your eyes again."

He tipped her face up and their gazes collided.

Her breathing hitched and her skin tingled everywhere. She was seized with the need to kiss and touch him. To follow all the pent-up emotions their reunion had stirred, leaving her aching for him for days on end.

"There it is." He ran his hands down her shoulders, dragging the only remaining strap of her dress off so the bodice slid loose to sag against her breasts. His eyes remained on hers, however. "There's that look I like. When you watched me walking into the surf tonight, you were staring at me with that expression in your eyes. It was all I could do not to haul you into bed like a caveman."

He turned her inside out with just his words while the heady scent of angel's trumpet and jasmine drifted on the warm breeze.

"I do that to you?" She leaned forward to press a kiss to his chest, savoring the smooth warmth of one pectoral. "I wish I'd known I had that power."

"Lydia." He skimmed a hand down her hair. Stroking. Petting. "You distract me too much already. If I told you everything you do that drives me crazy with wanting you, I'd never get anything done."

Through the veil of her hair, he toyed with the zipper at the back of her dress, flicking at the toggle and tracing the path it would take if he pulled it down. She thought she'd come out of her skin faster than she'd get out of her clothes, the slower pace making her flesh feel too tight and sensitive.

"You say that." She pressed another kiss to his chest, letting her tongue flick along the silken heat of smooth pectoral there. Then, gathering her courage, she arched up on her toes to speak softly in his ear. "But if I was anywhere near as irresistible as you claim, I'd be underneath you already."

With both her hands on his chest now, Lydia could feel the hard shudder go through him. Only then did she understand the restraint he was exercising.

"Is that what you think?" His hands pressed harder against her, molding her to him before he found that zipper again and started to ease it downward. "Because I was doing everything in my power to make tonight different than any time we've been together before. To give us a fresh start."

Her heart turned over in her chest even though she'd told herself a hundred times she wasn't going to let her emotions get all tangled up in this like last time. She couldn't go through that heartbreak again. Right now, she wanted to lose herself in pleasure, not think about a fresh start.

And yet…

How unexpectedly thoughtful of him to want to make tonight a new beginning. To make it different from their past together. She wanted to tell him that was unnecessary, but with the silk dress gliding lower and lower on her body, she found it difficult to argue with him. The sound of the sea rolling in provided a soothing music in harmony with the rustle of palm fronds, drowning out everything else as she shimmied the rest of the way out of her dress. The silk pooled at her feet, leaving her clad in the beautiful imported lace lingerie she thought he'd never see tonight.

"You're my wife now," he reminded her, backing her toward the bed while his blue eyes moved languidly over her body. They were both more visible now as they neared the bedside sconce. "Not just my lover. We should make tonight the start of something new. Different."

"I like that idea." She was breathless. So turned on she could hardly find enough air to speak. Underneath the coral-colored lace, her breasts tightened to impossibly taut peaks. "A new start, that is."

She remembered—vaguely—that she wanted their relationship to be different than before. So a do-over was a good thing. She could protect her heart from all the ways this marriage could hurt her before they said goodbye. But right now, she mostly wanted Ian McNeill all over her. Inside her.

He lowered her to the bed, her body meeting the soft duvet while Ian loomed over her, shirtless and golden in the torchlight. He unfastened his belt. She held her breath.

"But, Ian?" She chewed her lip as he freed himself from his trousers, her eyes sliding to the gray silk boxers that couldn't conceal how much he wanted her.

"Yes, wife?" He bent over her on the bed, brushing a kiss over one hip, his lips working a decadent magic on her skin.

"We don't need to make *everything* different than it was before." She remembered multiple orgasms—the first of her life. And then there was the tireless lovemaking that woke her in the middle of the night and left her sleeping more deeply— happily—than ever before.

She felt his lips smile against her hip while he kissed her there, and then licked a path along the hem of her lace underwear.

Her eyes might have crossed before she closed them, giving herself over to him.

"No?" He kissed. Licked. Kissed again.

Behind her eyelids, she was already seeing stars just thinking about what he might do next. Her body tensed with anticipation.

"No. Some things were really quite perfect." She debated shouldering her way out of the strapless lace bra top holding her in, the fabric like a straitjacket when she wanted to feel nothing but Ian's body against hers.

Her breath came in short pants. She licked her lips. Wriggled her hips. Arched her spine to get closer to him because she needed him. Now.

"Perfect." He repeated the word in a whisper over her skin, trailing a kiss into the indent of her waist as he covered her with his body.

Finally. Finally.

A moan of satisfaction hummed through her as the hard length of him pressed at the juncture of her thighs. She dragged him down to kiss her. She nipped his lower lip, unable to stay still beneath him. She couldn't get close enough, her breasts flattening against the hard wall of his chest in a delicious caress that left her wanting more.

The humid air hung heavy on her skin and his too, a salty ocean tang that made the night feel all the more exotic but familiar, as well. Like the past, but different.

When his mouth closed on her breast through the soft lace, she twined her fingers in his hair. Held him close and clung to the sensations he loosed in her with each flick of his tongue. He unfastened the series of hooks at the front until she could sidle free of the confining fabric. She slid one leg around his, wanting him everywhere.

He must have guessed, or else he was as caught up as she was, because he skimmed a touch between her thighs, teasing over the damp lace until she shuddered with the small convulsions that were a precursor to all the pleasure that was to come. She remembered this wildness, the heated, primal joining that had overwhelmed her in the past.

As Ian tugged aside the thin scrap of panties to find her slick core, Lydia forgot everything but the way he made her feel. Mindless. Sensual. Wanted.

With each stroke of his fingers, each press of his palm against her, the tension in her body coiled more tightly. He wound her up, taking her higher. She gripped his shoulders. Breathed his name.

And flew apart in a wave of orgasms that washed over and over her. It was even more amazing than she remembered. A blissful retreat from the world to a place where only pleasure remained. She reeled with the aftershocks for long moments knowing the night was only beginning.

Soon, he would be deep inside her. Joined with her physically to make their marriage legal. Binding.

As he poised above her, his body taut with a hunger he hadn't appeased yet, Lydia had just enough wits about her to wonder how she'd ever survive the onslaught of pleasure while guarding her heart. She walked an emotional tightrope tonight and—possibly—for many nights to come.

Heaven help her, she couldn't stop if she tried.

Ian needed her with a fierceness that defied logic.

Beads of sweat popped up along his brow. He ground his teeth together against the ache of it all.

He'd waited this long to take her. He could wait another minute to chase the sudden shadows from her gaze.

"Look at me," he commanded, unable to soften the edge in his voice. Instead, he simply lowered the volume.

His gaze met hers. There were definitely shadows there. The light was dim, but he knew the nuances of those green eyes. Time hadn't dimmed his memory of this woman's moods.

"I want you," she said simply. Urgently.

Was she running from her shadows by losing herself in this night with him? He was too amped up to figure out what might have upset her, but he knew she wanted him, too. She couldn't hide that.

"That's going to happen soon," he promised, already clutching a condom in one hand. "But I never gave you the proper kiss to commemorate the day."

Her eyebrows lifted.

"There were kisses," she argued, lifting her neck to plant another on his cheek, to one side of his mouth. "I was there for a lot of highly memorable kisses just now."

"Not a 'you may kiss the bride' kind of kiss." He let go of the foil wrapper, setting it beside the pillow near her head, where dark hair spilled in every direction.

She was so damn beautiful.

"I'm not sure how that kind is any different."

Frowning, she seemed appropriately distracted from whatever had bothered her a moment ago.

And that made holding back worth it, even if he throbbed as though a vise were clamped around him.

"I put it off before because I wanted to get it right." He wanted her to be happy on her wedding day, and he wanted to be the one to banish those shadows in her eyes. Call him old-fashioned, but even if it was a temporary marriage, Lydia was now his wife. She deserved something to mark that occasion—something more than the courthouse visit. "It didn't seem like the kind of kiss to share in front of strangers."

Her eyes locked on his. Curiosity mixed with desire. And he was damn glad he'd taken this moment to remind them both what it meant to be together tonight. Digging under the covers, he found her left hand and held it, running his finger over the platinum band and square-shaped diamond there. He twisted it gently—back and forth a few degrees in either direction before resettling it right where it had been. Resting it there anew.

Then, his gaze lowering to her lips, he kissed her. Savored her. He felt the tension ease out of her as her arms went around him. She returned the kiss with a sweetness that almost made him forget everything else that had passed between them.

And before he let himself think about that, he

retrieved the condom and rolled it into place. Never breaking the kiss, he made room for himself between her thighs and pressed deep inside her. Her fingernails scored his chest, scratching lightly as he found a rhythm that pleased them both. Heat flared all over, building gain until it roared up his spine with new urgency. He'd put this off too long. Forced himself to wait and wait. So now when the pressure built, it powered through him with an undeniable force.

He wrapped Lydia in his arms, rolled her on top of him so he could watch her. She bit her lip, her dark hair spilling over her shoulders as she moved in time with him, her narrow hips rocking in time with his.

He remembered so much about her and he used it to his advantage now, recalling exactly where to touch her to send her spiraling into ecstasy. He reached between them, fingering his way to where she was slick with heat. She arched back, still for a moment, before she collapsed over him, her body convulsing all around him. The soft, feminine pulses were his undoing, the feel of her pleasure spiking his own.

Their shouts mingled with the night birds and howler monkeys, a wild coming together that pounded through both of them. When the spasms slowed and stopped, Ian turned her in his arms so they lay side by side, breathing the same humid air of the Costa Rican jungle while the bamboo fan blades turned languidly overhead.

Their marriage was real now. The words they'd spoken in front of the county clerk were only a precursor to this, the ultimate bond that made it legitimate. He had been prepared to wait to consummate the marriage until she was ready, but maybe Lydia had seen that their union could have as many benefits as they allowed themselves.

Tonight might be a shadow of what a real marriage between them could have been like. But he could take a whole lot of pleasure from more nights like this. Whatever had driven her into his arms tonight, Ian wasn't about to argue.

Nine

Seated at the polished stone patio table across from Ian two hours later, Lydia decided she preferred dining while dressed in one of the T-shirts and boxer shorts he'd packed for their trip. Wrapped in a cotton throw blanket that she'd found on the back of the couch, she tucked sock-clad feet beneath her while Ian filled their water glasses from the pewter pitcher, still cold all these hours after they should have eaten.

But the caterers had left several covered trays of food with small candles burning in the stands below them on the buffet, while other dishes had been placed on ice, so everything she'd put on her

plate remained delicious. She helped herself to another bite of the baked pineapple that was so good
she couldn't wait to recreate it at home. Or maybe
everything simply tasted better after multiple orgasms. She didn't think she could shake the plea-
surable feeling in her veins if she tried.

Even knowing her marriage was utterly unorthodox and it wouldn't last beyond this time next
year, Lydia was determined to savor the joy of the
night. There would be worries enough when they
returned to the real world.

For now, eating cold lobster at midnight overlooking the Pacific with a fascinating, handsome
dinner companion, she couldn't muster the energy to worry just yet. The heady scent of flowers wafted on the sea breeze, and she reveled in
how her cooling skin was still warm from a shared
shower with Ian.

She flushed just thinking about the things he'd
done to her under the shower spray. But better to
think about that than the moments when he'd toyed
with her wedding ring and kissed her as though she
would be his bride forever.

"More wine?" he offered, lifting the decanter
of pinot grigio.

With his jaw shadowed by stubble and his dress
shirt unbuttoned to his waist, Ian still managed to
look completely at home at the formal dining table,
his blue eyes hooded from the glow of the candela-

bra that had remained burning thanks to the glass globes around the tapers.

"No, thank you." She took another drink from her water glass. "Being in Miami and now here, I'm thirstier than usual from the heat."

Or else she was thirstier than usual from the unaccustomed physical activity. Sweet, merciful heaven, but the man could do incredible things to her.

"Do you usually stay in Manhattan over the summer?" he asked as he bit into a slice of fresh mango. It was an innocuous question but one that reminded her of the differences in their worlds.

"Unless a client hires me for a job outside the city, I'm always in Manhattan." She shifted the cotton throw on her shoulders and tucked closer to the table. "I can't afford to get used to the Mc-Neill lifestyle."

All around the deck, tiki torches still burned. The animal life had quieted some so she could hear the roll of waves onto the beach below along with the ever-present swish of palm fronds in the breeze.

Ian frowned. "We have a house in the Hamptons. You could go there on the weekends if you'd like to escape the heat."

"That's just what I mean." She remembered how many times her mother had dragged her to Newport in the summer, couch-surfing with any potential acquaintance while she tried to wrangle an invitation from Lydia's father to stay at the Whitney mansion. "I don't want to get in the habit of living beyond my means."

He wiped his hands on a linen napkin and set it aside, then moved to take the seat next to her at the round table. Just his physical nearness affected her, spiking her heart rate the same way it had every single time he got close to her. It had been this way last year when she'd fallen for him. It had stayed that way even when she'd been angry with him and told him they were finished. Right to the last minute when he'd walked out of her hotel room in Rangiroa, she'd felt the hum of response to his nearness.

"Lydia, we'll be sharing my home in New York. You need to be comfortable there." He took her hand, threading his fingers through hers. "Our marriage needs to be believable."

She stared down at their interlocked hands, wondering what was for show now. His touch? His kiss? She needed to remember that they had a relationship based on mutual needs. Ian's legal need to keep the family business in family hands, and her need to protect the secret of Mallory West so she could continue her more lucrative side business of matchmaking to help struggling mothers. Simple.

And yet it would be so easy to let the chemistry she shared with this man distract her from her goals.

"I don't need to start spending weekends in the Hamptons to have people believe our marriage is real." She plucked a plump berry from a bowl of fresh fruit and took a bite. "Even if we were wildly in love and planning our forever, I wouldn't suddenly quit my job and give up my work with Moms' Connection."

"But you can expand your role there now." He leaned back in his seat, keeping her hand in his and resting their joined palms on his knee while the candelabra candles burned down a little more, dripping wax on the linen tablecloth. "Maybe chair your own fund-raiser for the group when we return to New York."

The possibility shimmered like a beautiful mirage. Help her favorite cause? Aid the women who had given so much to her those weeks when she'd been thinking she would be a single mother to Ian's child? She could do so much good there.

Except that it wouldn't last. Her time as a New York socialite would be short-lived.

"That's what I mean, Ian. In twelve months' time, I won't have the kind of social standing needed to chair Manhattan charity events. If anything, my reputation might very well be in a worse state than ever, and that's saying something considering my past."

"Then take a one-year position on their board. Do what you can to further their goals in that time.

All I'm saying is, it would be good to get involved at the level people would expect of my wife." He turned her shoulders toward him so she faced him head-on. "You might as well work with a group you support anyhow."

"Thank you." She couldn't deny the idea intrigued her. "It's generous of you to suggest."

He shrugged like it wasn't a big deal to write a substantial check to a group that struggled for every dime. "You'd be doing the legwork, not me. Besides, I'd like to find ways for you to be happy over the next year." A wicked grin slid over his face. "Outside of bed, I mean. Because that much I believe we have covered."

He drew her forward, his eyes intent on hers before he closed them at the last moment. He nipped her lower lip, and then soothed the spot with his tongue, sending a shiver of pleasure all over her body.

He hadn't been kidding about making her happy in bed. Ian McNeill had that power locked down.

"What about when we go back to the real world?" she asked, her eyes fluttering open. "I'm concerned you may have underestimated the level of interest the press will take in this marriage. Not to mention the interest my mother will have."

"We'll deal with that as it comes," he said firmly. "For now, if you're finished with dinner, I'd like my dessert."

The heated look in his eyes turned her blood molten.

"What about mine?" She pushed the words past lips gone dry.

"You'll get yours, Lydia McNeill," he whispered in her ear before licking along the lobe, his hand already seeking the hem of the T-shirt she wore and tucking underneath it. "That much I promise you."

An hour later—after much taste-testing of the dessert menu and his wife—Ian counted himself a lucky man. The marriage might be fake, but Ian was confident he was having as rewarding a honeymoon as any groom on the planet.

He sure as hell had a hotter wife than anyone else.

He had convinced Lydia to join him in the oversize hot tub off the master suite, another space that was mostly open to the elements. The sinks and bathroom had been situated on an interior wall, but the shower and hot tub could be partially exposed to the villa's private patch of forest on the steep mountainside that led down to the beach. With no other accommodations for miles, the Honeymoon House was the perfect blend of seclusion and luxury, with services available from the local resort.

Ian had shut down all the outdoor torches now that it was well past midnight. The house was quite dark except for the moonlight spilling across the hot tub's surface and the spa light underwater.

He watched as Lydia stripped off her T-shirt. His T-shirt, actually. He liked seeing her in his clothes. And he really, really liked seeing her out of them. He couldn't take his eyes off her now as she looked back over one shoulder before slipping a thumb into the band of the boxer shorts she'd folded over and tucked to fit her slender frame.

It didn't matter that the shadows were thick around them. He could see the shape of her hips as she wriggled free of the cotton. And, damn, he could see her even better as she faced the tub and hurried—naked—into the bubbling water.

Her high, firm breasts hid just beneath the surface. For a moment he wondered why he'd suggested this since what he really wanted was to bury himself inside her all over again and the hot tub was only going to slow him down. But then, this was her honeymoon, too. And he wanted to make sure he made their time here unforgettable for her.

She was already worried about returning to the real world and facing their families, which reminded him what a good, generous woman she was. He didn't want her to worry about any of that when he could take care of everything. She was his to protect now. He planned to erase all those concerns tonight before they slept.

"It's your turn," she called from the water, her

glossy, dark hair spilling around her like a mermaid in the clear bubbles.

"Just admiring the view." He stripped off his shirt that he had hadn't even bothered to button, tossing it onto the wood planks of the deck.

"So am I." She leaned back against one of the neck rests of the molded spa. "Feel free to take your time."

"You saying things like that makes it all the tougher to take my time. I hope you know that." He eased his shorts off, his body ready to go again from just looking at her.

Though her playful words only amped him up more.

"Maybe I like cracking that legendary McNeill control." She watched him as he stepped down into the tub beside her. Her pale skin was a liquid shadow in the water.

"Legendary?" He gathered up the hair floating around her and laid it over her shoulder. "You overestimate me."

"Do I? I've heard you're as coolheaded in the boardroom as you are on the job site—never rattled, utterly restrained, and it's impossible to guess what you're thinking."

Is that how she saw him?

He studied her pretty face washed clean of any makeup, her lips still deeply pink without any added color. Her eyelashes were dark and spiky from the water. And she studied him as thoroughly as he did her. It amazed him they didn't understand each other better.

"I'm actually more of the negotiator of the family. The link between my two brothers, who make a habit of taking the opposite views on just about everything." If he and Lydia were going to spend this year together, it might help if they knew each other better outside the bedroom. "Far from being the guy with legendary control, I'm the one most likely to do the compromising."

She arched her eyebrows and smiled. "Ian McNeill? Compromise? I can think of a whole host of independent contractors working on the luxury hotel in Rangiroa who would have been astounded to hear it. For that matter, most of my colleagues at work on the Foxfire are already nervous about the possibility of budget overruns."

"That's not necessarily a bad thing." He wondered if she was overstating the case. "I respect deadlines and budget constraints. I expect the people who work with me to follow suit."

"And they rush to do just that. All I'm saying is that you're not the easiest of bosses. I can't picture you as the one in your family who compromises."

That bugged him, actually. He forced himself to lean back against the seat though, unwilling to let her see as much.

"My whole life, I've been the one in the middle.

In age as well as temperament." He reached for her, lifting her legs and laying them across his lap so she was now sitting sideways in her corner seat. "When Quinn wants a highbrow hotel launch and Cameron thinks we could hit the youth market with a launch during Comic-Con, I'm saddled with finding the halfway point. And that's been true since the time Quinn was old enough to build a soap box derby car and spent all day painting it black with silver stripes, only to wake and find Cameron had used decoupage to paste 'artful nudes' all over the body."

She only half smothered a laugh. "I'd love to hear your compromise on that one."

"Before or after Quinn broke Cam's nose?" That had been the first of some ugly fights. They'd learned to work around each other—and respect their very different approaches—since then. But the learning curve hadn't been pretty. "I tried repainting the car, but since I was only eight at the time and had to paint over decoupage, it lacked the cool refinement of Quinn's version."

Lydia was quiet for a long moment. Feeling that he'd failed to bring the right touch of humor to the story, Ian wished he'd kept it to himself.

"Perhaps not getting your own way in the family dynamic made you all the more disposed to dictating the terms in your life." She tipped her head up to the moonlight for a moment, giving him a tempting view of her long neck and damp shoulders.

But her words had distracted him even more than her body. Did she have a point?

He filed the notion away, unwilling to lose this time with her by getting caught up in their differences.

"What about you?" He turned the tables, only because it was the first conversational tidbit that occurred to him and he didn't want to start analyzing his own situation. "No one defaces your prized possessions when you're an only child."

She tensed, a reaction he felt where he stroked her calves under the water.

"I wasn't, though." She straightened in the tub, but didn't turn away from him or move her feet off his lap. "My mother made sure I was very aware that I had half siblings and that my father treated them very differently from how he behaved with me."

"Damn. I'm sorry, Lydia." He sure as hell hadn't meant to stir up old hurts.

"No." She shook her head and waved a hand as if she could brush aside his concern. "Don't be. I think she hoped throughout my entire childhood that Dad would swoop in and raise me for her, but that never happened. Once she realized that she was going to have to be my mother—well, I was mostly grown by then. But we got along better once

I stopped expecting her to be a mom and started enjoying her as a friend."

"Yeah?" He massaged her feet, hoping to ease away the tension that had crept into her body since he started this conversation. He hated to think she'd never been her parents' number one priority. "Maybe I ought to try that approach with Liam. He was the nonparent in my youth. But at least I had my mother and grandfather."

"Although you were the one standing between your siblings when they came to blows." Her green eyes pinned his for a moment before shifting lower. "Maybe that's why you and I ended up getting along so well. For a few incredibly memorable weeks, we put one another first."

Until they didn't.

He wondered if that realization echoed through her

with the same dull ache that it did for him. But Lydia was already shifting closer, her naked thighs straddling his on the hot tub seat and making it impossible to think about anything but her. Them.

This moment.

Lydia needed to lose herself in Ian.

She didn't want to think about how much it had hurt when he put his family before her. When he'd refused to see how painful it might be for her that he'd allowed his grandfather to collect potential bride prospects for Ian when she thought she'd been the most important woman in his life.

All he had to do was deny it. Or explain it. But he'd done neither, drawing a line with her that she had been too hurt and angry to cross.

But even though a year apart had done little to soothe the raw, empty gap he'd left in her life, she was able to breathe all that hurt away enough to kiss his damp shoulder. To plaster her hands to his bare chest and absorb the hard warmth of his strong body. Selfish?

Maybe.

Or maybe there was a tenderness underneath that cold control of his. And maybe she'd kiss her way to it this time.

She could feel the moment when the fire that burned her caught him, too. His body came alive beneath her. His fingers flexed against her lower back, hands palming her spine and drawing her hips closer to his. Her thigh grazed the thick length of his erection, the contact making him groan with a hunger that reverberated through her, too.

"I want you." He said the words even though she understood as much from every single touch on her body.

"Not in here," she cautioned, her too-brief pregnancy coming to mind and causing a fresh pang in her chest.

"Too risky." He spoke into her ear, his hands

wrapping around her waist and lifting her higher against him. "I know."

In a flash, he had her on her feet, with him following her. A moment later, he stepped out of the tub and opened the warming drawer full of fresh towels, a billow of dry heat spilling out along with the scent of detergent and lavender. He turned back to her before she'd even stepped all the way out of the spa and extended a towel for her to wrap herself in.

Rather, he wrapped her in the towel and his arms, too. He already had one around his waist and one on the deck where they stood. She couldn't touch him back since her arms were pinned to her sides in the towel, but she arched her neck for his kiss, getting lost in the man and the moment.

Just the way she'd wanted. And better.

"Where should I take you?" He asked the question against her cheek as he trailed kisses there, down her jaw, and onto her neck.

Her whole body came alive for him, like it always had when he touched her. Every single time.

"Anywhere," she murmured, not caring as long as he kept touching her.

When he stopped kissing her, she opened her eyes a moment to see him gather up a stack of more towels before he took her hand and tugged her out on the deck toward a teak porch swing covered in gold-and-turquoise cushions. Gossamer-light mosquito netting was draped over it and there was a table full of hurricane lamps to one side of the swing, which looked like a pasha's bed. Ian paused to light two of the lamps before pulling her into the netting enclosure with him. He tossed the towels into one corner of the bed, a foil packet sliding off to one side.

She smiled at his careful thought to protection, a sweet gesture that made her relax against him as he pulled her underneath him.

"I can't get enough of you." He breathed the words into her skin as he kissed his way down her body, sliding aside the towel and licking over her sensitive breasts.

His thigh pressed between hers, the welcome weight hitting the place where she craved his touch most. Her back bowed off the cushions, hips meeting his despite the lingering barrier of the thick terry cloth at his waist. She tunneled her fingers through his damp hair, holding him to her, feeling the tension build deep inside her.

Still warm from the hot tub, her skin heated to a dull sheen from the humid air. She tugged at the remnants of the towels between them, needing to get rid of all barriers to having him deep inside her.

He touched her before she could finish the job, however, his hand covering her sex and moving in a slow circle that made her head loll back against the cushions while ribbons of pleasure stroked her from the inside. Helpless at that touch, she held herself very still, not wanting to miss the slightest movement of his fingers over the slick warmth.

When he slid a finger inside her, she went mindless, boneless with a melting desire. Delicate convulsions fluttered through her, one after the other, drowning her in sweet fulfillment.

"Please," she urged him. "Please, please. Right now." She patted around the cushions in search of the condom.

Seizing upon it, she clutched it in her fist and passed it to him. But there must have been two, because he already had one in place. She'd been too intent on her own mission to notice his.

He rolled her on top of him and she forgot all about it. He thrust into her and it was all she could do to remain upright. She held very still for a long moment, getting used to the feel of him. Relishing the way they moved together.

A tightly perfect fit.

Ian gripped her hips and held her in place, moving beneath her. She met each thrust, closing her eyes to lose herself completely.

The tension built again, the rapid pace of it catching her off guard. She steadied herself against his shoulders, her hair falling forward to stroke his chest while he moved faster. Harder.

Her release blindsided her before she was ready. Before she knew it would happen. It rolled over her, through her, again and again. She collapsed against him while his climax overtook him. She kissed his shoulder. His face. Whatever she could reach as the pleasure spent itself and their heartbeats quieted.

Slowly.

For long moments she simply listened to Ian's ragged breathing, liking the way the feelings played havoc with him, too. It helped to know she wasn't alone in this. That she affected him as much as he did her.

The force of it, the raw power of the attraction and the chemistry, was unlike anything she'd ever experienced. Unlike anything she knew could transpire between a man and a woman.

Maybe a small part of her had hoped that this marriage would show her that she'd been wrong about how monumental their relationship had been. If anything, being back together with Ian now only proved that they were more combustible than ever before.

The problem with combustible heat?

It didn't tend to burn itself out quietly.

Ten

By noon the next day, the honeymoon was over.

Ian regretted leaving Costa Rica, but Lydia kept saying she was worried about their families' reactions to the secret marriage. So, wanting to keep her happy, he'd arranged to leave, and now here they were, back on a chartered jet. It touched him that she seemed as concerned about the McNeills as she was about her own mother's response. And, of course, she had a legitimate reason to be concerned about how the tabloid media would choose to spin the story given her unique past. Whatever gossip played out online would be best quieted by a press release of their own.

So shortly after noon, they boarded the same private plane that had delivered them to Central America. The plan had been to return to Miami—and the Foxfire renovation project. But they had the aircraft at their disposal for the day and their bags packed with enough clothes for several days. So Ian needed to speak to her about a change of travel plans that he hadn't wanted to mention previously.

A change of flight plans he'd given to the pilot the night before.

He slid into the soft leather seat beside her, taking her hand before she could boot up her electronics for the trip. He understood she was anxious to check on the media reports about their marriage, but first he needed to clear a side trip with her.

No longer dressed in the honeymoon garments he liked so much—his T-shirts or the silk dress knotted at the knees for wading in the ocean—Lydia was now wearing a peach-colored linen sheath that reached her knees with an ivory jacket buttoned over it. With her dark hair pulled back in a neat ponytail and a heavy gold necklace, she had returned to work mode. His beautiful, endlessly competent wife.

"I've asked the pilot to give us a moment before takeoff." *Damn it*. Ian should have brought this up sooner. He'd been too busy enjoying what they'd shared this weekend—the connection and spark he remembered from their early days together. He'd wanted to lose himself in that when he knew damn well they would never return to the time when they offered one another a tenuous trust. Love.

Thinking about the betrayal of that trust—on both sides he could now acknowledge—still burned his gut.

"Why?" Lydia straightened in her seat, immediately alert. "Did you leave something behind?"

"No. Nothing like that." He took both her hands in his, hoping he'd earned back some small amount of her trust during this weekend together. They'd need that to make it through this marriage. "I wanted to speak to you about a possible change in our travel plans today."

She tipped her head to one side, more quizzical than upset.

"You know as well as I do the pilot has to file any alterations to the flight ahead of time—" She cut herself off, understanding lighting her features along with a new coolness. "Of course you know that. You've already changed our plans, haven't you?"

Ian could change the itinerary back again. They'd just need to wait until the plan was approved. He gripped her hands tighter, hoping she'd understand.

"Remember when I told you my brothers contacted me on the flight here yesterday?" At her nod, he continued, "They didn't check in just to let me know the news of our marriage had leaked. Apparently my grandfather has asked to see us— all of his family—as soon as possible. My brother said it wasn't cause to interrupt the honeymoon, but the sooner we could come to New York for a family meeting, the better."

"Is it his health?" The look in her green eyes was compassionate. Concerned.

Something about that quick empathy soothed the raw places inside him.

"I don't know. I would have thought I'd be able to tell by my brothers' faces if they were worried about him. But honestly? I couldn't read them. I don't know if they're putting up a brave front because we just got married." The fear had been in the back of his mind for nearly twenty-four hours and it was a relief to share it.

To feel Lydia squeeze his hands in return.

"Of course. We'll go straight to New York. There's no work in the world that's more important than a loved one's health."

Her reaction humbled him. Even as he gave the nod to the pilot and settled in for takeoff, he recognized that he'd missed out on something special with this caring woman. What might have happened if he'd swallowed his pride last spring and forced her to listen to his explanation about why his profile was circulating on a matchmaker's website even as he dated her? If he'd fought harder for her—hell, fought for her at all—could he have made her see the truth? That he hadn't given a rat's ass about anyone but her?

In all the months since their breakup, he'd been too busy blaming her for believing the worst of him. For not having any faith in him.

But maybe he'd been every bit as guilty as her. More, even.

The realization made him wonder if he could use these next months to turn this marriage into something real. Convince Lydia that they were meant to be together after all.

He was still brooding over the idea when Lydia's soft expletive hit his ears—an unlikely exclamation from the woman who had cultivated a perfect facade to keep scandal-hungry tabloid reporters at bay.

"What's wrong?" He glanced over at her as the plane began to taxi toward the runway to begin the flight.

Lydia squeezed her phone in a white-knuckle grip.

"It's my mother." She shook her head, slowly leaning back in the leather chair with a sigh that blew her dark hair from over one eye. "She's already lining up press interviews for us." Lydia turned an anguished look his way. She caught her lip between her teeth for a long moment, worrying away the slick peach lip gloss. "She wants to meet

me at a network television studio in New York tomorrow for a live interview with one of the morning shows." Lydia drew in a long breath. "The host
already shared her lead-in to the story." She flipped
the phone so he could see a text from her mother
in all capital letters.

BILLIONAIRE'S REJECTED LOVE CHILD FINALLY
HITS THE JACKPOT AS A MCNEILL BRIDE!

Six hours later, seated beside Ian in a chauf-
feured limousine transporting them from the private New Jersey airstrip to Malcolm McNeill's
residence on Park Avenue in Manhattan, Lydia
talked herself through her plan for getting through
this day. Ian had taken a business call to handle a
few details on the Foxfire Hotel project in South
Beach, leaving Lydia alone with her thoughts for
their ride through the city.

For which she was grateful.

Trying to steady her trembling hands and jittery
nerves, she sipped the bottled water stocked in the
limousine's mini bar. The events of the last day and
a half had been staggering. Her wedding. Finding
out the event had been leaked to the press. The
unbelievable honeymoon night in Costa Rica. An
unexpected trip to New York because Ian's grandfather wanted to meet with his whole family.

Her mother's sudden interest in her life now that

Lydia had tied the knot with one of the wealthiest men in the country.

Lydia's stomach churned as the limo stopped at a red light. Ian had been kind about her mother's meddling notes and eager desire for involvement in her life. He had reassured Lydia that she understood she wasn't responsible for her mother's behavior and promised her that the McNeills would deal with any media stunts her mother pulled.

In the end, Lydia had opted not to contact her mother just yet. For all that Mom knew, Lydia remained on her honeymoon for the next week or more. She had no reason to believe Lydia was back in New York and all too close to the network studio where her mother had committed to an interview.

Lydia thought she was done with this kind of thing—trying to manage her mother's need for the spotlight while staying firmly out of it herself. She hadn't factored in this kind of thing when Ian had offered his proposal for a marriage that would benefit both of them.

Sliding a sidelong glance at him now as the car turned into Central Park and headed east, Lydia braced for the swell of desire that just a simple look inspired. His dark suit was more casual today with his white dress shirt open at the neck. His legs were sprawled, one knee close to hers, his left hand resting on his navy trousers, the platinum wedding band glinting in the sunlight.

She thumbed her own ring as she watched him, her eyes greedily moving over his strong jaw and the dark hair that brushed his collar. Her heart tumbled over itself in an odd rhythm, alerting her to the presence of all the old feelings for him. The ones she wanted so desperately to ignore. The ones that tingled along her senses even now at just sitting near enough to touch him.

When he'd kissed her the night before and told her he wanted them to have a fresh start, she'd felt her defenses tremble. And today, after she'd read the texts from her mother and she'd been hurting and embarrassed on so many levels, Ian had been quick to assure her he could handle any of her mother's media antics, promising to hire a full-time publicist to manage Lydia's image and ensure that the media knew whom to contact for all stories having to do with Lydia McNeill.

It had sounded so smart and reasonable, and it probably was a very real possibility that his solution would work. It helped to have the financial resources, of course. But more than anything, the gesture had spoken of a kindness and consideration for Lydia's feelings that rocked her old perceptions of him.

Had she been too quick to judge him last year? Too insecure in herself to ever believe that Ian might have a reasonable explanation for his presence on a matchmaker's site? Her gaze returned to his platinum wedding band as he finished up his call. He might have pressured her into a marriage that would help him fulfill his grandfather's wishes, but he was helping her at the same time. She couldn't afford the scandal or the financial strain of a legal battle with Vitaly Koslov.

Another kindness Ian had done for her sake.

"I wonder what you're thinking, Mrs. McNeill." His words cut through her daze as the limo emerged on the east side of Central Park.

Startled, she sat bolt upright on her seat, her drink sloshing droplets on her arm. She set the water aside in the cup holder to give herself time to gather her thoughts. When had he finished his phone call? She needed to get her head on straight before they walked into his grandfather's house and faced the full contingent of McNeills. Ian had phoned his brothers from the plane to let them know they were flying to New York earlier than anticipated. Apprehension flitted through her, and Lydia wished she'd taken Ian up on his offer of a light lunch during their flight to New York. Maybe having something in her stomach would have helped ease her nerves.

"Just a few jitters about meeting all the McNeills at one time." She smoothed the hem of the peach-colored dress some anonymous staffer of Ian's had packed for her back in Florida before this trip. She really needed to find out more about him and the people who worked with him, who'd made this trip just a little less stressful by sending some of her own clothes with her. "I know you said that your family trusts your judgment so they will accept your choice of wife, too."

"They will see what I see. A smart, compassionate woman who's battled complicated obstacles to carve out a good career." He took her hand and lifted it to his lips, his blue eyes warm.

Would she ever get used to the way he made her pulse flutter like that?

Then she recalled the whole reason for this trip and cursed herself for becoming sidetracked by her own worries. "But I'm being selfish." She shifted to face him on the bench seat, her knee grazing his. "You have much deeper concerns than that for this visit. More than anything, I hope your grandfather is well."

"Me, too," he said simply, turning to peer out the window as the driver slowed the car. "But we'll know soon enough how he fares because we're here."

Lydia marveled as they came to a stop at the curb outside a six-story limestone building with an Italianate facade and a delicate wrought iron balcony off the second floor. Her designer's eye went to the clay-tiled mansard roof and neo-Renaissance details, but it was difficult to enjoy the beauty of one of New York's turn-of-the-century masterpieces when Ian's family was on the other side of the front door.

No matter what Ian said, she worried what his brothers would think of their unorthodox—and rushed—marriage. But right now, she needed to be there for Ian in case his grandfather's health had taken a turn for the worse.

Resisting the urge to pull a mirror out of her purse and indulge the old insecurity demon her mother had given her, Lydia took a deep breath and stepped out of the vehicle as the chauffeur opened the door. She would remain calm. Composed.

Strong.

Ian had been all of that and more for her in the face of her mother's attempted publicity stunt.

The iron gates of the foyer rolled open before Ian announced them on the intercom. Clearly, they'd been expected.

"I texted Gramps's housekeeper," Ian explained as they strode into the house without knocking. "She must have been watching for us. She said my brothers are here. Sofia is running late because of a ballet performance earlier in the day, but she's due to arrive shortly."

He closed the door behind them and Lydia did her best not to gawk. She'd read that Malcolm McNeill was an avid art collector, but she hadn't expected to be greeted in the foyer by a Cezanne and a Manet. The pieces were hung to be enjoyed, with the focus on the art. The only piece of furniture was a settee in a shade of cerulean shared by both paintings. Lydia had seen the opposite approach often enough in her time as a designer—boastful collectors who were more interested in having their taste admired and envied.

"Wow." She'd been drawn to the pieces in spite of herself, only realizing after a long moment that Ian was speaking in quiet tones to someone off to one side of the hallway.

Lydia turned to join them, but the older woman in a gray uniform had already hurried away.

"Cindy tells me the family is upstairs," he informed her, pointing the way. "It's two flights to the library, though. Let's take the elevator out of deference to your shoes." He cut a quick sideways glance her way. "Though they make your already-gorgeous long legs look damn amazing."

Before she could think of a response to his outrageous compliment—that yes, she did enjoy—he was already pushing the call button, and the elevator door swished open. She followed him into the cabin. The grand staircase snaked through all six floors with a mammoth skylight at the top, and though beautifully impressive, she didn't relish the idea of testing her heels on the sleek, polished treads. Not that she planned to take them off and walk in to meet Ian's grandfather barefoot.

As the door closed behind them, whisking them

upward, her apprehension grew. But Ian stepped nearer, and the warmth of his physical proximity somehow comforted her.

"Thank you for coming with me." He spoke with quiet sincerity. "I'm glad you're here."

The words so perfectly echoed what she'd been feeling at that moment, they slid right past her defenses and burrowed in her heart in a way that made her breath catch.

Before she could think what to say, Ian folded her palm in his and squeezed. "We might as well hold hands." He planted a kiss on her temple. "We're newlyweds, remember?"

The soft warmth of his lips stirred a hungry response in her as she recalled their honeymoon in vivid, passion-saturated detail. But as the full import of his words sank in, she wondered if the display of affection was for his family's sake more than anything.

The elevator cabin halted and the door slid open on a third-floor hallway flooded with light from the skylight over the central staircase. Male voices and laughter sounded from nearby. Ian led her to a partially closed door flanked by carved wood panels that were flawless reproductions in the French eighteenth-century style. Better to focus on the home design than the butterflies in her stomach.

"That's my grandfather's voice," Ian noted, walking faster. "He sounds good."

Lydia squeezed his arm, offering what comfort she could as she followed him into a library where the walls were fitted with historic Chinese lacquer panels between the windows overlooking the street. But not even the superb design details could sway her attention from the impressive men scattered around the room. Even before introductions were made, she knew she was seeing three generations of McNeills. The gray-haired eldest sat in a leather club chair in the corner. Wearing a retro red-and-black smoking jacket belted over his trousers, the patriarch of the family gripped a crystal tumbler half-full of an amber-colored drink, a forgotten copy of the *Wall Street Journal* tucked into the chair at his side. At the window stood an extremely fit man who looked to be in his late fifties. He'd shaved his head completely, and she could see a tattoo on the back of his neck. Was this Liam McNeill? His gray pants and black T-shirt combined to make him look more like hired muscle than Ian's father.

But as the middle-aged man turned toward her, she saw the same ice-blue eyes shared by every man in the room.

Ian introduced her to each member of his family in age order, ending with Quinn and Cameron, who rose from their seats on opposite ends of the room to greet her.

Quinn and Cameron, she thought, looked more

alike than Ian, whose bronzed complexion favored their Brazilian mother. But Cameron was very tall, perhaps six foot five. She would have thought him a professional athlete if she'd seen him on the street.

Lydia was saved from making small talk by the arrival of an exquisitely beautiful, petite blonde, hair tightly coiled in a bun at the back of her head.

"I'm so sorry," the woman offered, rushing to Quinn's side. "I thought the train would be faster since traffic was ridiculous after the show, but there were delays." She kissed Quinn. Her eyes darted around the room and, finding Malcolm McNeill, she moved to give the older man a kiss on one cheek that coaxed a smile from him.

"Sofia, my new wife, Lydia." Ian repeated his simple introduction from earlier.

Lydia braced herself for a chilly greeting since she'd unwittingly stolen some of the woman's wedding thunder with their preemptive visit to the justice of the peace, but if Sofia Koslov resented it, she hid it well.

The ballerina winked at Lydia, although she remained at Quinn's side as he guided her to a love seat at the center of the room.

"I've been so eager to meet you." Sofia pulled a silver phone from her small leather hobo purse and waved it. "Let's exchange numbers before you leave."

"I'd like that." Lydia couldn't help smiling, feeling more at ease with another woman in the room full of accomplished, powerful men. She and Ian took a seat on the long couch opposite Quinn and Sofia.

Without preamble, Malcolm McNeill reached for his silver-topped cane and rose to his feet, every bit as tall as Ian, even with his bent knees and back. "Lydia, we're all glad to welcome you into our family." He lifted his glass in a silent toast and took a sip before returning it to the side table. "I hope you will consider a more public celebration this summer so we can show the world how pleased we are to call you a McNeill."

The old man's blue eyes pinned her, inciting gratitude for the warmth of the gesture even as she regretted deceiving him. All of them.

Ian squeezed her hand as if he guessed her thoughts.

"Thank you, sir." She ducked her head, oddly intimidated to be in the hot seat in this room full of strangers who would be her family for such a short time.

Luckily, she didn't need to worry about saying anything else, because Malcolm continued to speak.

"It's Liam who asked me to round up the whole lot of you." Malcolm looked over to his son and gestured to the room. "Go on now. Tell 'em."

"Dad wanted us all here?" Ian rose to offer

his grandfather an arm while the older man lowered himself into the large club chair. "Gramps, I thought you called us together to talk about your health. How you're doing since the heart attack and the trip home from Shanghai."

"No, no." Malcolm McNeill waved aside the help and the concern. "I'm healthy as a horse."

Lydia felt the unease all around the room in the shifting of positions. Cameron sat forward in his chair, elbows on his knees.

He then scowled at his father. "Dad, what gives? Ian left his honeymoon for this. Sofia ditched her meet and greet after a ballet performance."

Liam cleared his throat. "It's not easy getting you all together at once." He strode around to the desk, staying on the perimeter of the room, rubbing a hand over his shaved head. "My apologies for the timing, but I've waited long enough to tell you about this."

Quinn spoke up. "That sounds ominous, Dad." The oldest of the McNeill sons turned in his seat to better see his father. Quinn was a hedge fund manager, Lydia knew, and had all the appearances of refinement and wealth. But then, at the end of the day, that's what he sold—access to a world of privilege by gaining the trust of the world's wealthiest investors.

Cameron sighed. "What gives?" the youngest

asked again, spreading his hands wide, a note of impatience in his voice.

Ian remained silent at her side.

Then Liam McNeill stopped pacing the perimeter of the room and turned to face the rest of the family. Lydia held her breath.

Liam looked around the room at all of them before speaking. "I have another family I've never told you about. Three more sons, actually." A ghost of a smile flitted across the man's face before vanishing. "Your mother left me because she found out about them, but I could never convince Audrey— my other, er, girlfriend—to move to the States and be a permanent part of my life."

The news landed with all the force of a grenade, sending shrapnel into the heart of every McNeill. And that was before Cameron McNeill stalked across the room and launched a fist into his father's jaw.

Eleven

Ian hauled a steaming Cameron to one side of the library while Quinn stood in front of their father, blocking further physical confrontation. They might as well be a freaking reality TV show at this rate. *McNeills Gone Mad!*

Ian couldn't believe he'd left his honeymoon and flown to New York for this news, let alone that he'd dragged Lydia into it. Lydia—a woman who had lived her life as carefully as possible to avoid big, messy scandals. He noticed that Sofia had moved to sit beside Lydia on the couch, the two of them silently on the same side without saying a word.

What was it about women that they could remain civilized when all hell broke loose around them?

Even Quinn looked the worse for wear after the dustup, with his shirttails untucked in front and jacket unbuttoned. Ian hadn't fared as well; struggling with six-foot-five inches of pissed-off muscle and impulsiveness had sent him through the wringer. While epithets flew back and forth, it became apparent that Liam had been cheating on Ian's mother for years, fathering sons with a mistress on the West Coast until the woman got fed up with his refusal to divorce his wife and left the United States the year after Cameron was born.

Private investigators had trouble finding her, but then she'd had years of McNeill money stashed to help her make the getaway. Liam had lost touch with her and his sons until a few weeks ago, when one of the old investigators snagged a lead on a McNeill family ring in a pawnshop in the US Virgin Islands. Liam thought it was just a ploy by the PI to resurrect an old job, but he'd contacted Ian's friend Bentley to track it down, and it turned out the ring was real, verified by a family jeweler. Bentley traced it to the servant of a wealthy family—named McNeill—in Martinique.

"They use our name?" Ian barked, feeling more than a little angry with his father himself.

Furious, actually.

"I don't know when the boys started using the

name," his father said, hanging his head. "But their mother died long ago and they want nothing to do with us, so you don't have to worry about anyone coming in here and…"

Quinn swore. Cam accused their father of several indecent acts. Ian's eyes went to Lydia, wishing she didn't have to hear all this. She looked calm, however, if a little pale. She held her cell phone in one hand; her other was tucked under her thigh on the couch.

"Quiet down, all of you, and listen here." Gramps stood, using his cane as he moved. "These young men are your half brothers, like it or not. They are your blood. My blood. Every bit as much my grandsons as you are. That doesn't mean, however, that I plan to give them the whole kit and kaboodle of the family portfolio." He straightened as much as his bad back would allow and used the cane to point at Cameron. "I've invited them to New York and we'll take their measure when they arrive."

Ian exchanged glances with Quinn. Family was all well and good. But what did this mean for them? And for McNeill Resorts if their grandfather handed over shares to people who clearly resented them? Ian didn't give a damn about money, but the family business they'd poured their blood, sweat and soul into? That was another matter. Let his fa-

ther do right by his offspring financially, sure, but
protect the business.

"Gramps, that's fine," Ian said reasonably, step-
ping on Cam's toe to ensure his brother didn't gain-
say him. "We understand you want to meet them
and provide for them. But what about McNeill Resorts? You've spent our whole lives trying to im-
part what the company means to you and how you
want it developed. You can't honestly mean to start
parceling off your business to people who are complete strangers to you?"

Out of the corner of his eye, Ian noticed Lydia
straighten in her seat. Belatedly, it occurred to
him she might feel differently about this newly
unearthed branch of the family. Hell, in her childhood, she'd been the unacknowledged heir, and it
had caused pain her whole life.

"I meant it when I said they're as much my
grandsons as you are." Gramps leveled a look at
each one of the brothers, a stiff set to his jaw, before he put his cane back on the floor and shuffled
toward the door. "Now that we have that out of the
way, I'm going to change for dinner. You're all invited, but don't stay if you can't act like grown-
ups." He paused at the door, almost running into
Lydia, who had leaped off the couch to open it
for him.

Gramps smiled at her. "You're a pretty thing,
aren't you? If it gets too rough in this room, just

head down to the dining room and someone will fix you up a cocktail." He patted her arm.

"Yes, sir." She beamed.

Gramps had made one person happy today. As for the rest of the McNeills, Ian couldn't imagine what this meant for the family. He'd just gotten married to secure his portion of his grandfather's company because he had been under the mistaken impression it meant so much to the old man.

Now? The whole damn trust and will were almost assuredly going to be rewritten to incorporate this new branch of the family their father had never bothered to mention.

That bugged Ian on a lot of levels—mostly because he had to contend with the news that his father was a selfish, cheating bastard. Yet what bothered him more than anything was the idea that if the will was altered and it no longer included a stipulation about taking a wife to secure a portion of McNeill Resorts, would Lydia suggest they dissolve their marriage?

You can't honestly mean to start parceling off your business to people who are complete strangers to you?

Ian's words echoed in Lydia's mind long after they left his grandfather's home. They chased around her brain even now, late that night, after they'd arrived at Ian's apartment at the historic

Pierre Hotel on Central Park, where both Ian and
Quinn owned space. They'd opted to spend another day in New York so that he would have time
to meet with his brothers and figure out what their
father's news meant for the family.

Lydia hadn't argued, understanding why he
would want to talk to his brothers privately. But
the events had shaken her. Ian had locked himself
in his library to make calls and Lydia found herself walking in aimless circles around the kitchen
at midnight.

She and Ian hadn't stayed for dinner with Malcolm after the McNeill family blowup. She understood why a meal together might be uncomfortable
with so much unsettled among them, but no wonder
she was hungry now. She rifled through the cabi-
nets in the sleek, caterer-friendly kitchen, search-
ing for food.

Lydia had said good-night to Malcolm McNeill
in his study while he drank his aperitif before going
in to dinner. Liam had left immediately after his father walked out of the library. Quinn and Sofia had
made their excuses as well, and Sofia had looked
strained, although she'd taken Lydia's number and
promised to call her so they could arrange a time
to get to know each other.

Cameron alone had remained behind to have
dinner with his grandfather. In the car afterward,
on the way to Ian's apartment, Ian had sincerely

apologized for the family dustup. But Lydia hadn't cared about that half as much as she cared about the fact that Ian didn't believe in welcoming half siblings into the family. He'd called those half brothers "complete strangers," implying they had no right to any McNeill inheritance.

He reacted the same way her half siblings had when they found out about her existence. It didn't matter that they all shared a father. She'd never been good enough in their eyes and it troubled her deeply to think Ian felt that way about people who shared his blood.

Peering into the huge Sub-Zero fridge, she retrieved a bottled water and sat at the breakfast nook overlooking the lights of Central Park. She'd changed into a nightgown and a white spa robe she'd found in the bathroom. Although Ian owned the Pierre apartment, apparently the whole building shared the hotel maid service and—come to think of it—Ian had told her there was twenty-four-hour room service from the kitchens downstairs. She would have phoned for something, but now, as it neared midnight, she tried to talk herself out of it.

Even all these years after that photograph of her in a magazine with a "baby bump" at sixteen, Lydia found herself careful not to overeat. Except, of course, in those weeks where she hugged the news of a real pregnancy close. Then, she'd fed herself like a queen, dreaming of the baby she'd never gotten the chance to meet.

"There you are." Ian's voice from the far side of the kitchen startled her from her thoughts.

He flipped on a pendant lamp over the black granite countertop. The backlight made it so she couldn't see out the window anymore. Instead, her own reflection stared back at her, a pale, negative image in black and white.

"Were you able to resolve anything?" she asked, careful to keep her thoughts to herself about any disappointment with Ian's reaction to his father's news.

It was possible the shock of the moment had colored his response. In time, he might feel differently about welcoming his half brothers into the family.

"Not really." He took a seat in one of the four white armchairs surrounding the polished teak table in the open-plan dining area. He set his phone on the table beside him. His shirtsleeves were rolled to expose strong forearms and he'd removed his jacket and tie. "I spoke at length to Bentley, the same friend who found you when I was looking for Mallory West. My father called him to go to Martinique two days ago and confirm the identity of my half brothers. Bentley said there's no doubt. He has photos of my father with his other family when they were young."

Ian switched the phone on and called up a photo

of Liam McNeill standing with one woman and three small boys in front of the Cezanne she recognized from Malcolm McNeill's foyer. The three boys had to be Quinn, Ian and Cameron—all three of them sweet and adorable in jackets and ties, but with mischief in their matching blue eyes.

Below that photo, was another of Liam with an obviously pregnant blonde in a long, white gauzy dress. They stood on a beach at sunset, the sky purple and pink behind them, their arms around two small boys who could have been twins to the three in the photo above. Same blue eyes, same grins. The only difference was that the boys in the beach photo wore white T-shirts and cargo shorts. She wasn't sure why the third half brother wasn't in the photo.

"I can't believe that no one knew about this." Lydia ran a finger over the woman's pregnant belly in the photo. Had she known about Liam's other family when she carried those children? "I think back to all the stories that ran about me as a teen—complete fiction. And yet your father successfully hid a whole double life from the tabloids."

"My mother knew about this." Ian slid the phone from her hands and turned off the screen, setting it facedown on the table. "She just didn't want our lives to turn into a media circus so she kept quiet about it when she left my father."

"Our mothers are cut from very different cloth,

aren't they?" Lydia wondered if he had any idea how much she identified with his father's *other* family. "I'm more surprised that his mistress didn't expose the truth."

Ian shook his head. "Maybe she had enough money. Bentley said the house where she raised her sons was paid for in cash."

Lydia drew a deep breath and reminded herself the shock of the news hadn't worn off yet for him. And still, she couldn't keep from pointing out, "It's not always about money. Most women want their children to have a relationship with their father. Don't you wonder why she cut off all contact and her sons never got in touch with the family either?" She turned that over in her mind. "As much as I resented the way my mother tried to get my father's attention by making us a spectacle, I wouldn't have had any relationship with him if she hadn't brought me to his attention."

And in the end, her father had been kind. He'd encouraged her desire to study art and design and introduced her to prominent people in the field in which she now worked. She'd found common ground with him and enjoyed those long, last conversations about beautiful buildings he'd seen all over the world. She treasured those memories.

"If not for that damned ring showing up, we might never have discovered them." Ian stared down at the table and she wondered if he'd heard what she'd said. "And now? Everything my grandfather worked for is going to land in the laps of people who never wanted anything to do with us."

She tried to bite her tongue. And failed.

"They're still your family," she reminded him. "That counts for something."

She wanted—*needed*—him to agree. Even when she had been pregnant with their child—a baby who would not have had the legal protection of marriage—she had thought Ian would embrace his offspring. That he would see beyond those rigid notions of what "family" meant. But if he truly believed that he could only count the legally recognized brothers as worthy of his notice...

Then she didn't know him at all. Then her marriage really was based strictly on a piece of paper and all those tender touches in Costa Rica were just a case of physical attraction.

He turned on her, blue eyes thoughtful. "How can you, of all people, believe that family trumps all? Your half siblings did everything in their power to discredit you and your mother when your mom sued your father's estate. How could you even consider them family when they've gone out of their way to hurt you like that?"

Disappointment prickled all over her, deflating the hope she'd had that Ian was a different kind of man. That they were building a tentative trust again.

"You can't pick family the way you choose your friends. But I still believe those relationships are worth investing in. If I hadn't gotten to know the Whitneys, I would have missed out on knowing my father." She stared down at the yellow diamond on her finger, more confused than ever about what it meant.

About what Ian hoped to gain by playing the part of her husband in a way that had fooled even her.

"Lydia, I'm sorry that this had to come up right now." He took her left hand and kissed the backs of her fingers. "I can see you're upset and I don't blame you. I'm going to order a tray for you from room service and have something brought up."

"There's really no need."

"I insist." The gentle concern in his eyes undid her as he stroked a thumb over the inside of her wrist, still holding her hand. "I haven't forgotten about your mother's attempts to reach you. And with your permission, I'll invite a publicist over tomorrow and you can plan how you want to manage the news about our marriage and your public image. The woman—Jasmine—is a good friend of Sofia's. Quinn highly recommended her."

"Thank you." Lydia slid her hand away, the diamond weighing heavily on her finger. "I appreciate that. But in all the events of the evening we haven't even spoken about what this news of your father's means for your grandfather's will."

A muscle in Ian's jaw flexed as he leaned back from the breakfast table. "It means nothing."

"Ian, it's not too late to say the wedding photo was—I don't know—a prank?" She held her breath while he looked back at her with stunned eyes. "I'm not trying to add to your problems, but if it simplifies things for you to quietly annul this, we could—"

"No." He bit off the word with a fierceness echoed by the flash of emotion in his eyes. "Absolutely not." He leaned over the table and kissed her—a hard, possessive kiss. "As much as I regret that you had to witness the whole drama with my father, having you with me was the only bright spot in this day."

Her heart contracted, squeezing hopefully around those words. She took a deep breath, no closer to answers than she had been hours ago. Before she could say anything he rose to his feet.

"I'll have the kitchen bring something up and then I've got a few more calls to make." He kissed the top of her head. "If the publicist is here at ten tomorrow morning, is that too early?"

"That's fine. I'll be ready." She knew she needed help figuring out how to manage her public image. Whether or not she stayed married to Ian for the rest of this year, she'd come to one decision tonight.

She'd allowed the fear of a scandal surrounding Mallory West to send her running into his arms for protection from a lawsuit, and that problem wasn't going to go away after twelve months.

Even if Ian ensured Vitaly Koslov never sought legal retribution, there was the fact that Lydia wanted to return to matchmaking. And aside from that one small scandal that she'd never addressed, her alter ego actually had a great, lucrative reputation.

More than ever after tonight, Lydia was convinced she had a mission in life to champion single mothers. Women who were ostracized by family or lovers who refused to recognize their own children.

So, at ten the next morning, she planned to ask Jasmine the publicist how to introduce herself to the world as the mystery matchmaker, Mallory West.

As for Ian? She didn't plan to consult him about that particular decision. She had every reason to believe he wouldn't understand.

Twelve

Two hours later, Ian paced the floor of his study, a restless unease still weighing on his chest even though he was checking things off his mental to-do list with reasonable speed.

He'd exchanged emails with the site manager on the Foxfire project and gotten an update on the South Beach property, a lucky stroke since the guy was as much of a night owl as him. Ian had triple-checked the marriage paperwork to ensure it had all been filed properly, then he faxed his attorney the signed files outlining the provisions Ian was making for Lydia no matter what happened in the next twelve months. She'd made it clear she didn't want any kind of financial settlement in a year's time—an issue he'd revisit—but for now, he made sure she received all the legal and financial protections possible as his spouse.

What she'd said at the kitchen table earlier still needled his brain and he didn't understand why. He had the impression she was unhappy with his response to his father's bombshell about his second family, but he couldn't quite put his finger on what he'd done wrong.

Sure, she'd made the comment that family wasn't all about money. But she'd also seemed upset that he wasn't welcoming the McNeill interlopers into his grandfather's company. And since Ian couldn't untangle what bothered her, he planned to make sure she knew that he didn't equate her position in the family with these pseudo McNeills.

Lydia's case was different. *She* was different. Special.

Ian made his last call of the night to Quinn, still hoping to dispel some of the tension of the day. He knew none of his brothers would be getting any sleep tonight either.

"I have Jasmine confirmed for tomorrow morning," he informed his older brother, who was probably staring out at this exact same view of Central Park three floors above him right now. "Thank you for the recommendation. She got back to me almost immediately."

"She's a go-getter." Quinn sounded weary on the other end of the call, but no doubt he'd been making calls well into the night too, trying to sort through the news of their half brothers. "Jasmine is very protective of Sofia and her image. They're friends, of course, but I got the impression that she's the kind of person who invests a lot in her clients."

"That's exactly what Lydia needs. Her mother has tried undermining Lydia's image too many times." It had upset Ian when he made a quick scan of articles about Lydia tonight—so he could give the publicist some background on the situation. "It will help her to have a go-between she trusts to manage the stories that circulate about her."

Lydia had a giving heart and a willingness to help people that was too rare in his world. She should be recognized for her efforts. Or, at the very least, not belittled by sensationalized stories that focused on her personal life.

"You'll be happy with Jasmine." Quinn paused a moment. In the background, Ian could hear the clink of ice cubes in a glass. "And I've been meaning to let you know that Sofia has told me twice to cancel any efforts to find Mallory West."

"Seriously?" Ian stopped his pacing, instantly alert.

"Yes. She mentioned it a couple of weeks ago, saying that we shouldn't hound someone who was responsible for bringing the two of us together."

Quinn's tone shifted as he spoke about his fiancée. There was a lightness that had been absent in him until Sofia arrived in his life. "I thought she was just being sentimental, or... I don't know. I didn't think she was serious about it. But last week she raised the issue again, and apparently she's already spoken to her father. So definitely call off any search for the matchmaker."

That was good news for Lydia.

And Ian was happy about it, too. One less thing to worry about that could chip away at Lydia's public image during a time when they were trying to cultivate a new one.

Yet he had to wonder. Would this give Lydia all the incentive she needed to end their marriage early?

"Ian? You there?"

"Yes. Sorry. I'm just surprised. But I'll abandon that project and call in the investigator." No use telling Quinn he'd already found Mallory and that she currently slept in his bed.

"Thanks. And don't be surprised if Sofia knocks on your door tomorrow morning. She has a ballet class to teach at noon, but she mentioned wanting to personally introduce your wife to her friend Jasmine before she heads in to work."

Distracted, Ian agreed to relay the message before disconnecting the call.

His brain was still stuck on the news that the

Koslovs no longer cared about finding the matchmaker who'd embarrassed them. Now Sofia had decided it was because of Mallory's matchmaking that she'd met Quinn in the first place.

Ian couldn't keep up. Shutting his phone off for the night, he padded barefoot through the apartment, heading to his bedroom. He craved Lydia's touch. Hell, she was most certainly sleeping already. Even just lying beside her would be enough to chase some of the restlessness away.

But as he stepped into the master suite, he knew right away that she wasn't there. Her suitcase had been moved from his closet where he'd set it himself earlier. His bed was still made.

Maybe she was still in the kitchen? Even as he stalked through the darkened apartment, however, he knew she wouldn't be there. When he passed the closed door to one of the guest suites, he knew she'd found an empty bed to sleep in for the night.

He placed a palm on the door, missing her. He told himself that she was probably just trying to get better sleep. This way, he wouldn't wake her when he went to bed. If that was her reasoning, he could hardly begrudge her the guest room. But the vague unease in his chest all evening took a new form. He'd been worrying about what his father's betrayal meant for the family when he should have been paying attention to Lydia.

He'd let her sleep for now. They would speak in the morning when they were both clearheaded.

Because deep in his gut he knew she hadn't sought that spare room for the sake of a good night's rest. His new wife wasn't happy with him. And more than ever, he feared that she was already dreaming up ways to end this marriage.

As Lydia prepared for her meeting with her new publicist the next morning, she nibbled on the scones that Ian had had delivered to the kitchen, along with a huge platter of other breakfast choices. If this was a real marriage, she would ask him about the possibility of rethinking some of his extravagant expenditures to help others. She could think of five struggling young mothers she helped through Moms' Connection who were probably going without breakfast today so their kids could have something nutritious. It made it hard for Lydia to enjoy the scone when so much food sat there untouched.

She hadn't seen Ian yet this morning. She'd awakened to discover he had a meeting with the McNeill family's private attorney. He had been in the study all morning.

So she prepared for her own meeting with the publicist by herself, asking the morning maid to set out the coffee and pastry treats in the living room to offer her guests. Because apparently Sofia Koslov would be joining them briefly, too, if only to make introductions. She'd texted Lydia this morning to make sure she didn't mind.

Already, Lydia had the impression she would have been truly fortunate to marry into this family for the sake of gaining a sister-in-law like Sofia. Lydia had read a great deal about the principal dancer for the New York City Ballet last winter during the awkward media coverage of Cameron's proposal to her. How would Sofia react one day when she learned that Lydia was actually Mallory West? The possibility of being rejected that way— by someone so warmhearted—stirred a deep regret for how she'd handled the matchmaking mistake.

What struck Lydia now, as she finished her scone and reviewed her notes for her morning meeting, was that Sofia Koslov must share some of Lydia's desire for family. The dancer's mother had died when Sofia was a girl, and she'd never been close to her father, even though the Ukrainian-born billionaire had stepped in to claim control of her life. But as Lydia read about Sofia, she couldn't help but think they might have really enjoyed being sisters.

Too bad Lydia's temporary marriage was proving even more temporary than she'd imagined.

She heard the apartment doorbell chime and checked her watch, guessing that it was Sofia since it wasn't quite 10:00 a.m. and Sofia was scheduled to arrive a little before Jasmine. Letting the maid answer the door, Lydia took another moment to freshen her lipstick and check the fall of her bright green summer dress with big purple flowers embroidered at the hem. She wore a thin yellow sweater around her shoulders to cover up the dress's square halter neck.

When she got to the living room, Sofia darted off the couch. Dressed in slouchy pants and a leotard with a hoodie thrown over it, she could have been a nineteen-year-old college student with her clean scrubbed face and glowing skin. Her still-damp hair was piled on her head in a bun with a braid wrapped around it. She moved gracefully toward Lydia, meeting her in the center of the room.

"You look so pretty!" Sofia exclaimed, taking in the embroidered hem of Lydia's dress. "You already dress like a publicist's dream. Jasmine is going to love working with you."

They made small talk for a few minutes, comparing notes on clothes, but before Lydia could offer her guest a seat, the door to Ian's study opened down the hall. The voices of Ian, Quinn, Cameron and a stranger echoed off the Italian marble floor.

"I forgot Quinn was coming down here for the meeting with their attorney." Sofia's smile was infectious, the grin of a woman in love. "He worked so late last night, and then was up at the crack of dawn. Not that I'm supposed to know that since I'm technically living in my own apartment until my wedding." She made a good-natured eye roll. "But how could I leave Quinn alone last night after what they had to deal with yesterday?"

Lydia felt a pang of guilt at Sofia's empathetic words. Should Lydia have kept more of her opinions to herself last night?

Her eyes went straight to Ian as the men walked into the living area, close to the private elevator. Their business conversation must be done, as they joked about their golf handicaps and a charity fundraiser at a popular course in Long Island the following weekend.

Cameron checked out of the guy talk early, his eyes landing on the plate full of pastries on the coffee table. He made a beeline for it as his brothers said goodbye to the attorney.

Cameron gave Lydia a thumbs-up before speaking around a mouthful of jelly doughnut. "This must be your doing. Ian never has food in this place. Good job."

"I'm glad someone is enjoying it." She smiled in spite of the tension knotting her shoulders at Ian's arrival in the room. Something had shifted between them last night and made her uneasy today. She had slept in another room, but he hadn't spoken to her about it—last night or this morning. Had he thought it peculiar? Or were they back to being strangers with a contractual marriage?

Quinn and Ian joined them in the living area. Sofia and Quinn drew together like magnets, each pulled toward the other irresistibly, splitting the distance between them to meet in the middle. It was beautiful—and painful—to see, making Lydia realize all that she'd sacrificed in tying herself to a man who didn't think in terms of love and family, but business and legal obligations.

Sofia tucked her head to Quinn's chest. "Quinn, did you tell your brothers that we don't want to pursue any investigation into Mallory West?"

Lydia gasped. She covered it with a cough and a murmured, "Excuse me."

She was careful to avoid Ian's gaze, although she felt it on her.

Thankfully, Cameron McNeill spoke over her gaffe. "Are you kidding me? I thought we were going to sue her for all she's worth and donate the money to one of Sofia's favorite charities?" He leaned down to the coffee table to scoop up another pastry and a napkin. "I thought it was a great plan."

Ian was suddenly standing by Lydia's side, his arm sliding beneath her lightweight sweater to palm her back. "Quinn told me you no longer wish to pursue the matchmaker. I've called off the investigator."

When? And had he planned on telling her that the Koslovs no longer cared to sue Lydia's alter ego? She tensed beneath Ian's touch, anger tightening every muscle.

"May I ask why?" Lydia asked, not caring if they all thought her rude to question them about a piece of private family business.

She needed to know. Why had Ian let her think that the lawsuit from Sofia's father was still very much a possibility? Had he been that intent on marrying her to fulfill his grandfather's will? Her chest burned with frustration and her stomach rebelled at the scone she'd eaten earlier.

Sofia smiled warmly. "Of course. I was never upset with Ms. West after I discovered it was my father's matchmaker who truly caused all the trouble with me getting paired with Cameron." She gave a sisterly elbow to Cameron's stomach as he stood beside her. "But I made a point of speaking to my father about it last month and convinced him that there was no need to scare a good matchmaker out of practicing her skills in New York. I mean, thanks to her—and Olga, the matchmaker my dad hired—I found Quinn."

How kind of Ian to let me know.

Lydia felt breathless and immobile, kind of like she'd had the wind knocked out of her. Behind her, she felt Ian's grip tighten on her waist, but she knew that as soon as his family left, she would tell him what she'd known yesterday and hadn't wanted to admit to herself.

She could not possibly stay married to him.

Thirteen

From a leather slipper chair in the corner of the spare bedroom, Ian watched—stunned—as Lydia packed her few things an hour after Jasmine left the apartment following a tense meeting. He'd only stayed for a portion of it, sensing he was the one causing the tension for Lydia. But he'd been able to see for himself that Jasmine had things well in hand for managing Lydia's public presence, making smart suggestions for how to handle Lydia's mother all the while maintaining control of all publicity.

He hoped she was simply preparing for their flight to Miami to return to work on the Foxfire. He feared it was more than that since their plane wasn't scheduled to take off for nine more hours.

Lydia folded a white silk nightgown with unsteady hands, her focus overly careful. "How long have you known that the Koslovs didn't plan to sue me?"

Her words hung in the air. She smoothed the neatly folded garment on the bed, then tucked it into the small travel bag she'd set on a nearby luggage valet. Her face was still averted. She looked too pretty in her bright dress, and he wished he could twirl her around the room and make her smile the way they had in Costa Rica.

And before that, in Rangiroa.

What was it about their relationship that it only seemed to thrive in vacation mode? He should've never returned to New York with her so soon.

"Quinn told me to call off the investigator last night in a phone call after you'd gone to bed." It was the honest truth.

But it wouldn't be the first time she'd ignored the truth to draw her own conclusions.

She gave a vague nod, hearing his words, but never slowing her pace as she moved to the closet and found the next item of clothing to fold—the sheath dress she'd worn yesterday.

"You didn't have any inkling that your family no longer cared about uncovering Mallory West's identity?" She glanced his way, her green eyes huge and rimmed with red, before she returned to her task. "I asked Jasmine about my double identity in confidence, and she said—if I want her to—she would speak to Sofia about having us reveal the truth together and turn it into a story of happily-ever-afters." Lydia's voice hitched on the phrase and she stopped. She swiped an impatient hand across her cheek as she refolded the dress that wasn't cooperating. "She said it could be the perfect publicity spark to relaunch Mallory's matchmaking career, especially if Sofia were to get behind the Moms' Connection charity."

Ian hated to see Lydia hurt and upset. He wanted to wrap his arms around her and comfort her. Remind her that she knew him better than that.

But she'd never had faith in him, assuming the worst of him when his profile had landed on a matchmaker's site last summer. Assuming the worst of him now, even though he'd told her the truth. That's why he'd kept this marriage agreement *flexible*.

Smart of him, right?

So why did he feel as though her leaving was driving a knife through his chest?

"I had no idea that Sofia had talked her father into giving up the search for Mallory West," he reiterated, hoping if she heard it clearly, a second time, the words might mean more to her. "Lydia, I will tell you honestly that I was confident once I spoke to Vitaly Koslov and told him I knew Mallory's identity and that she meant no harm, he would forget about pursuing legal action."

"Yet you used the threat of a lawsuit to maneuver me into a marriage that would secure your share of McNeill Resorts." She straightened from folding the clothes and faced him. "That in itself seems…disingenuous."

"Perhaps," he conceded. "But don't forget that when I came to Miami to speak to you, I thought you'd been playing revenge games with me by matching me up with inappropriate people through your matchmaking service." He cut her off before she could argue. "Only you weren't. I jumped to that conclusion about you, not realizing you'd just lost our child and were hurting desperately. And I am sorrier for that than I can ever say."

He rose from the chair, needing to hold her. Hoping she would let him.

"It seems we are both at fault for misjudging each other," she admitted, her voice thin and her expression unhappy. "But I was in the same apartment as you last night when you found out that your family had forgiven me for the matchmaking mistake. You could have told me then, or this morning."

"It would have been easy to do if you'd been in my bed, where I thought you'd be." He wondered why he hadn't knocked on the door to the guest room last night. Asked her what was wrong and shared that good news with her.

Maybe he really hadn't wanted to know that she sided with his new half siblings over him. That once again, he didn't come first with someone he loved—

Loved?

He let the word settle in his head, into his heart. And yes, hell, yes, he realized he loved her.

That's why his chest hurt as though it wanted to bleed out on the floor at her feet. He loved Lydia. And she was already looking for a way out of his life. Again.

"I wasn't half a globe away, Ian. I lay wide-awake in a bed one hundred feet from yours," she reminded him, tears gathering in her green eyes. "I guess I thought after the way our honeymoon went, maybe you wouldn't always have to put the McNeills before me."

He reached out to her, clasping her shoulders in his hands.

"You are a McNeill, damn it." He'd spent half the evening making sure she was legally protected in every way.

But Lydia was already tugging off her wedding ring. She held it out to him, the yellow diamond winking in the afternoon sunlight slanting in through the curtains.

"Not for much longer, Ian." She dropped it into

his hand, and it was only then, when he held the cold stone in his palm, that he realized his hands had fallen from her shoulders.

"We still have months together," he informed her, his tone fiercer than he intended.

How could he convince her to make this a real marriage unless she stayed with him?

"It's not too late to admit we made a mistake." She turned her back on him, her green dress swishing as she moved around the room, taunting him somehow. "I thought I could pretend with you for twelve months and somehow survive the emotional fallout, but after how close we got in Costa Rica, I know I can't do that. I can't pretend when it hurts this much."

"And you're not worried about a scandal now, when a divorce after a three-day marriage will put you in the headlines for the rest of the year?" He hated himself for saying it.

Especially right on the heels of realizing he loved this woman. He should let her go with some dignity, damn it. Except he'd tried that once before and it hadn't made him any happier.

"I've realized a scandal is far less painful than a broken heart." She snapped the suitcase closed. "I called for a car, Ian. I'm going to stay at my place and see Kinley before I return to South Beach. I'll send someone up for my bag."

She picked up her purse and walked out of the

guest room while Ian scraped his heart off the floor.

Wait a minute.

Why would *her* heart be broken?

He tried to put the pieces together and figure out what she meant. Why she was so upset.

Bloody hell.

Just as the elevator doors shut behind the woman he loved, he realized the truth that should have been obvious ever since they'd peeled each other's clothes off in Costa Rica.

She loved him, too.

By some kind of miracle, Lydia rode the elevator all the way down to the first floor without crying.

She hadn't wanted to walk through the busy lobby past the concierge desk with tears streaming down her face. She'd spent too much of her life trying to avoid making a scene to let herself fall apart publicly.

She hadn't called for a car. That had been total fiction she'd made up for Ian. And she didn't send someone up for her bag the way she'd told Ian she would. The tears behind her eyes were burning, burning, burning, so she blindly hurried out of the Pierre and rushed toward the closest traffic light so she could cross Fifth Avenue and lose herself in Central Park. A sea of tourists crowded the Grand Army Plaza, but she bypassed all of them, feeling the tears already plunking from her eyelashes to her cheeks.

Hugging her purse tighter, she squeezed through a line of city visitors waiting to ride the Big Bus. Couples and families milled around the food vendors, some checking street maps and others negotiating prices with the hansom cab drivers.

Lydia's shoes clicked along the pavement and onto the shady road leading into the park down to the pond. She found an empty bench near Gapstow Bridge, close enough for her to enjoy the view as well as some privacy. Only then did she give in to the crushing feeling in her chest, letting loose a soft wail of sadness that only constricted her lungs more.

Damn him.

She rummaged for tissue in her purse and came up with an antique handkerchief she'd purchased in a vintage shop a year ago. She'd washed it and tucked the linen in her bag, but hadn't found reason to sob her heart out in public until now.

She just couldn't see any reason to remain in a marriage with a man who freely admitted he only wanted to wed her to legally protect his share of a family business. But now, with the news of his half siblings and his grandfather's need to rewrite his legal documents to include the rest of the family, Ian didn't need her to serve that role anymore.

Plus, she didn't need Ian's protection from a lawsuit since that wouldn't be happening either.

They'd been hasty. And she'd been too entranced by his kisses to see what a bad idea it was to play house with a man who held your heart in his hands. She'd been foolish.

She'd loved Ian McNeill ever since that first night together in Rangiroa.

"Is this seat taken?" The familiar masculine voice came from over her left shoulder.

She debated her options for running and hiding. She did not want Ian to see her like this. Sniffling loudly behind her handkerchief, she gave an inelegant shrug and tried to collect herself.

"Lydia, I need to talk to you." He lowered himself to the bench beside her.

She felt the warmth of his knee graze hers, but he didn't touch her otherwise. She ducked her head, unwilling to meet his eyes. How on earth had he found her? He must have followed her.

"I feel like you had your say back in the apartment, but I didn't really get to make my case." He draped a hand along the back of the metal bench, but didn't touch her. "I'd like a chance to tell you a few things before you follow through with…whatever you decide to do."

She was going to have their marriage annulled. That was her plan. But she hadn't recovered her voice yet from the crying. And she couldn't deny she was curious.

"I have not been myself for the last twenty hours—ever since I learned about the way my father betrayed my mother. Let me just start by saying that much. I know that I upset you last night, but I was too caught up in the family drama to chase down why, and I regret that. Deeply." He moved closer. "There is no McNeill more important to me than you. Not my brothers. Not my half brothers. And yes—there will be a difference for me until I meet the McNeill doppelgängers in person and decide what I think about them."

She heard a big group of people coming down the path near the bench and wiped her eyes on the handkerchief, not wanting to look like a basket case. But her ears were closely attuned to what Ian was saying. She was surprised he'd come after her at all.

"I swear to you, I didn't know Vitaly Koslov was going to drop the idea of a lawsuit when I proposed to you. I may have hit that angle hard to convince you to marry me, but I genuinely believed he would sue you. Cameron is working closely with Sofia on a new ballet video game, and he's mentioned more than once that bit about suing Mallory West so Sofia could use the proceeds for a charity that helps bring art and dance to underfunded school systems." Ian drew a breath, pausing as the large group of tourists walked past, led by a private tour guide still giving statistics about the Gapstow Bridge's reconstruction.

The pause gave Lydia time to process. Sofia and Cameron were making a video game? Not for the first time, she wished she could have been a part of the family. A real part.

She'd never had that, always on the outside looking in.

"Anyhow, I had every reason to think Sofia's father would make good on that threat until Quinn told me otherwise last night." Beside her, Ian traced a flower on the hem of her dress where the fabric lay between them on the bench. That part of the full skirt didn't touch her body, but still…

The small action felt intimate.

Her heart ached.

"I believe you," she blurted before she'd even planned to speak. "That is, I already regret the way I didn't hear you out about why you were on a matchmaking website last year. I was hasty and misjudged you then, and I'm not making that same mistake again." If only that was the extent of their problems. She shifted beside him, finally daring to turn and face him. "But, Ian, you can't deny that you deliberately put a time limit on our relationship. That you tied up our relationship with a contract because you had no interest in a real marriage."

"A fail-safe," he said simply. "I fell in love in Rangiroa, Lydia. I wanted you to marry me then and bought this ring a whole year ago." He produced the yellow diamond from his pocket. "When you said you never wanted to see me again…it crushed me. But not so much that I pawned the ring."

Her heart tripped over itself, and then lodged somewhere in her throat. She swallowed hard, her smile wobbly with love. And hope.

"You've had the ring—all that time?" It didn't compute. Even when she'd been miscarrying alone? Even when he'd found her in Miami and maneuvered her into a fake marriage?

"Yes, although I have to confess, I couldn't look at it for months." He held it up to the sunlight and the smaller stones ringing the yellow diamond refracted light in a dazzling pattern. "But when I went to South Beach—a job I took specifically because I knew you were working there—I brought the ring with me and thought I'd see what happened."

"But you wanted a contract. You said it was only temporary." She thought back to that day on the rooftop of the Setai when it felt as if she had no options but to say yes to him.

"How many times could I risk breaking my heart on one woman? Or at least, that was the logic I used then." He took her left hand in his and stroked over the finger where the ring once rested. "But after what we shared in Costa Rica, after having you fall asleep in my arms again, I knew that my heart is yours to break, Lydia. However many times it takes."

Emotions swelled and burst inside her. She had to clutch a hand to her chest to keep them all in. But she couldn't hold back a shocked gasp as he handed her the ring again.

And then he got down on one knee in front of the bench in Central Park for all the tourists to see.

"Will you marry me, Lydia? For real, and forever? I love you, and if you think you can love me, too, we can say our vows again in front of our family. All of them." His lips curved in a smile more compelling than that gorgeous, one-of-a-kind diamond. "Even the Caribbean McNeills, if you want."

She could sense people nearby stopping and staring. It was the first time in her life she didn't mind being a spectacle.

"Yes." A half cry, half laugh hiccupped out of her throat. She nodded fast. "Yes, Ian. I will marry you again and again. I'm far too in love with you to do anything else."

All around them, people clapped. Whistled. Cheered. The whole tour that had passed them before had stopped to watch the Central Park proposal.

Lydia let Ian slide the ring onto her finger, and

then hauled him up onto the bench to kiss him, not caring who saw.

When he stopped, he whispered in her ear, "You think your publicist will mind we didn't clear this with her? I'm pretty sure there were some cameras around."

"I'm returning to matchmaking," she whispered back, her heart swelling with happiness. "I need to show I can at least get it right for myself."

Ian leaned away to look in her eyes and cupped her cheek in his hand. "You just made your first customer the luckiest man on earth. If you want, I can give you a testimonial."

She couldn't withhold a grin. She traced a finger over his mouth and watched heat flare in his blue eyes. "I'd rather have an encore."

To his credit, he didn't hesitate.

* * * * *

COMING NEXT MONTH FROM

HARLEQUIN
Desire

Available July 3, 2017

#2527 THE BABY FAVOR
Billionaires and Babies • by Andrea Laurence
CEO Mason Spencer and his wife are headed for divorce when an old promise changes their plans. They are now the guardians for Spencer's niece...and they must remain married. Will this be their second chance, one that leads to forever?

#2528 LONE STAR BABY SCANDAL
Texas Cattleman's Club: Blackmail • by Lauren Canan
When sexy former rodeo champion turned billionaire Clay Everett sets his sights on his spunky secretary, he's sure he holds the reins in their affair. Until he learns Sophie Prescott is carrying his child. Now all bets are off!

#2529 HIS UNEXPECTED HEIR
Little Secrets • by Maureen Child
After a fling with a sexy marine leaves Rita pregnant, her attempts to reach the billionaire are met with silence...until now! Brooding, reclusive Jack offers to marry Rita—in name only. Will his new family give him the heart to embrace life—and love—again?

#2530 PREGNANT BY THE BILLIONAIRE
The Locke Legacy • by Karen Booth
Billionaire Sawyer Locke only makes commitments to his hotel empire—until he meets fiery PR exec Kendall Ross. Now he can't get her out of his mind—or out of his bed. But when she becomes pregnant, will he claim the heir he never expected?

#2531 BEST FRIEND BRIDE
In Name Only • by Kat Cantrell
CEO Jonas Kim must stop his arranged marriage—by arranging a marriage for himself! His best friend, Vivian, will be his wife and never fall in love, or so he thinks. Can he keep his heart safe when Viv tempts him to become friends with benefits?

#2532 CLAIMING THE COWGIRL'S BABY
Red Dirt Royalty • by Silver James
Rancher Kaden inherited a birth father, a powerful last name and wealth—none of which he wants. His pregnant lover, debutante Pippa Duncan, has lost everything due to a dark family secret. Their marriage of convenience may undo the pain of their families' pasts, but will it lead to love?

SPECIAL EXCERPT FROM

⬡ HARLEQUIN®
Desire

*When billionaire boss Cameron McNeill goes
undercover in a tropical paradise to check out his
newest hotel's employees, he doesn't expect to want to
claim beautiful concierge Maresa Delphine and her
surprise baby as his own...*

*Read on for a sneak peek at
HIS ACCIDENTAL HEIR
by Joanne Rock*

As soon as he banished the hotel staff, including Maresa
Delphine, he'd find a quiet spot on the beach where he
could recharge.

Maresa punched a button on the guest elevator while
a young man disappeared down another hall with the
luggage. Cameron's gaze settled on the bare arch of her
neck just above her jacket collar. Her thick brown hair
had been clipped at the nape, ending in a silky tail that
curled along one shoulder. A single pearl drop earring
was a pale contrast to the rich brown of her skin.

She glanced up at him. Caught him staring.

The jolt of awareness flared hot and unmistakable. He
could tell she felt it, too. Her pupils dilated a fraction,
dark pools with golden rims. His heartbeat slugged
heavier. Harder.

He forced his gaze away as the elevator chimed to
announce their arrival on his floor. "After you."

He held the door as she stepped out into the short hall. Cameron used the key card to unlock the suite, not sure what to expect. So far, Maresa had proven a worthy concierge. That was good for the hotel. Less favorable for him, perhaps, since her high standards surely precluded acting on a fleeting elevator attraction.

"If everything is to your satisfaction, Mr. Holmes, I'll leave you undisturbed while I go make your dinner reservations for the week." She hadn't even allowed the door to close behind them, a wise practice, of course, for a female hotel employee.

The young man he'd seen earlier was already in the hall behind her with the luggage cart. Cameron could hear her giving the bellhop instructions.

"Thank you." Cameron turned his back on her to stare out at the view of the hotel's private beach and the brilliant turquoise Caribbean Sea. "For now, I'm satisfied."

The room, of course, was fine. Ms. Delphine had passed his first test.

But satisfied? No.

He wouldn't rest until he knew why the guest reviews of the Carib Grand Hotel were less positive than anticipated. And satisfaction was the last thing he was feeling when the most enticing woman he'd met in a long time was off-limits.

That attraction would be difficult to ignore when it was imperative he uncover all her secrets.

Don't miss
HIS ACCIDENTAL HEIR by Joanne Rock,
available June 2017 wherever
Harlequin® Desire books and ebooks are sold.

www.Harlequin.com

HARLEQUIN® *Desire*

AVAILABLE JUNE 2017

A TEXAS-SIZED SECRET

BY *USA TODAY* BESTSELLING AUTHOR

MAUREEN CHILD,

PART OF THE SIZZLING
TEXAS CATTLEMAN'S CLUB: BLACKMAIL SERIES.

When Naomi finds herself pregnant and facing scandal, her best friend steps up. He claims the baby as his own and offers to marry her, in name only. But his solution leads to a new problem—she might be falling for him!

AND DON'T MISS A SINGLE INSTALLMENT OF

TEXAS CATTLEMAN'S CLUB:
BLACKMAIL

No secret—or heart—is safe in Royal, Texas...

The Tycoon's Secret Child
by *USA TODAY* bestselling author Maureen Child

Two-Week Texas Seduction by Cat Schield

Reunited with the Rancher
by *USA TODAY* bestselling author Sara Orwig

Expecting the Billionaire's Baby by Andrea Laurence

Triplets for the Texan
by *USA TODAY* bestselling author Janice Maynard

A Texas-Sized Secret
by *USA TODAY* bestselling author Maureen Child

AND

July 2017: *Lone Star Baby Scandal* by Golden Heart® Award winner Lauren Canan
August 2017: *Tempted by the Wrong Twin* by *USA TODAY* bestselling author Rachel Bailey
September 2017: *Taking Home the Tycoon* by *USA TODAY* bestselling author Catherine Mann
October 2017: *Billionaire's Baby Bind* by *USA TODAY* bestselling author Katherine Garbera
November 2017: *The Texan Takes a Wife* by *USA TODAY* bestselling author Charlene Sands
December 2017: *Best Man Under the Mistletoe* by *USA TODAY* bestselling author Kathie DeNosky

HD83849

Turn your love of reading into rewards you'll love with
Harlequin My Rewards

Join for FREE today at
www.HarlequinMyRewards.com

Earn **FREE BOOKS** of your choice.

Experience **EXCLUSIVE OFFERS** and contests.

Enjoy **BOOK RECOMMENDATIONS**
selected just for you.

PLUS! Sign up now
and get **500** points
right away!

Earn
FREE
REWARDS
Join
Today!
HarlequinMyRewards.com

MYR16R

HARLEQUIN®
A *Romance* FOR EVERY MOOD™

Love the Harlequin book you just read?

Your opinion matters.

Review this book on your favorite book site, review site, blog or your own social media properties and share your opinion with other readers!

Be sure to connect with us at:
Harlequin.com/Newsletters
Facebook.com/HarlequinBooks
Twitter.com/HarlequinBooks

Whatever You're Into... Passionate Reads

Looking for more passionate reads from Harlequin®?
Fear not! Harlequin® Presents, Harlequin® Desire and
Harlequin® Blaze offer you irresistible romance stories
featuring powerful heroes.

♦HARLEQUIN® *Presents.*

Do you want alpha males, decadent glamour and jet-set
lifestyles? Step into the sensational, sophisticated world of
Harlequin® Presents, where sinfully tempting heroes ignite a
fierce and wickedly irresistible passion!

♦HARLEQUIN® *Desire*

Harlequin® Desire novels are powerful, passionate and
provocative contemporary romances set against a backdrop of
wealth, privilege and sweeping family saga. Alpha heroes with
a soft side meet strong-willed but vulnerable heroines amid a
dramatic world of divided loyalties, high-stakes conflict and
intense emotion.

♦HARLEQUIN® *Blaze*

Harlequin® Blaze stories sizzle with strong heroines and
irresistible heroes playing the game of modern love and lust.
They're fun, sexy and always steamy.

Be sure to check out our full selection of books
within each series every month!

Get 2 Free Books,
Plus 2 Free Gifts—
just for trying the Reader Service!

YES! Please send me 2 FREE Harlequin® Desire novels and my 2 FREE gifts (gifts are worth about $10 retail). After receiving them, if I don't wish to receive any more books, I can return the shipping statement marked "cancel." If I don't cancel, I will receive 6 brand-new novels every month and be billed just $4.80 per book in the U.S. or $5.49 per book in Canada. That's a savings of at least 8% off the cover price! It's quite a bargain! Shipping and handling is just 50¢ per book in the U.S. and 75¢ per book in Canada.* I understand that accepting the 2 free books and gifts places me under no obligation to buy anything. I can always return a shipment and cancel at any time. Even if I never buy another book, the 2 free books and gifts are mine to keep forever.

225/326 HDN GLPZ

Name   (PLEASE PRINT)

Address   Apt. #

City   State/Prov.   Zip/Postal Code

Signature (if under 18, a parent or guardian must sign)

Mail to the **Reader Service:**
IN U.S.A.: P.O. Box 1867, Buffalo, NY 14240-1867
IN CANADA: P.O. Box 611, Fort Erie, Ontario L2A 9Z9

Want to try two free books from another line?
Call 1-800-873-8635 or visit www.ReaderService.com.

*Terms and prices subject to change without notice. Prices do not include applicable taxes. Sales tax applicable in N.Y. Canadian residents will be charged applicable taxes. Offer not valid in Quebec. This offer is limited to one order per household. Books received may not be as shown. Not valid for current subscribers to Harlequin Desire books. All orders subject to credit approval. Credit or debit balances in a customer's account(s) may be offset by any other outstanding balance owed by or to the customer. Please allow 4 to 6 weeks for delivery. Offer available while quantities last.

Your Privacy—The Reader Service is committed to protecting your privacy. Our Privacy Policy is available online at www.ReaderService.com or upon request from the Reader Service.

We make a portion of our mailing list available to reputable third parties that offer products we believe may interest you. If you prefer that we not exchange your name with third parties, or if you wish to clarify or modify your communication preferences, please visit us at www.ReaderService.com/consumerschoice or write to us at Reader Service Preference Service, P.O. Box 9062, Buffalo, NY 14240-9062. Include your complete name and address.

HDI7